BEER
A Novel
By Thomas J. Hubschman

Published by Savvy Press
Salem, New York
Cover art by Eric Black

For my sons and grandchildren.

Savvy Press PO Box 63
Salem, NY 12865
http://www.savvypress.com/
ISBN : 978-1-939113-79-5

Other Books by Thomas J. Hubschman

Look at Me Now (Novel)
My Bess (Novel)
Song of the Mockingbird (Novel)
Father Walther's Temptation (Novel)
Billy Boy (Novel)
The Jew's Wife & Other Stories

I

I sit beside my father in a dark bar next to the 168th Street bus terminal on upper Broadway. Across the avenue, no Great White Way in this part of town, stands Columbia-Presbyterian Hospital. The American flag atop its gray tower, not the distant spire of the Empire State Building in the pink haze to the south, is the most prominent landmark I see through the bus's thick side window whenever my mother and I cross the George Washington Bridge from New Jersey to catch the "A" train down to Macy's on Herald Square. My mother's brothers will all eventually end up in Columbia-Presbyterian when their arteries become blocked from years of heavy smoking and drinking as members of New York's Finest. Two will die there. But this is still 1947, a hot Sunday afternoon when my uncles, like my father and mother, are still young, though of course I don't know that.

I sip my Coke and stare at the ranks of green and gold bottles standing in front of the mirror behind the bar, surely more alcohol than anyone could consume in a lifetime. My father is in the mirror as well, his eyes glazed by his first beer of the day. Right behind him is his double reflected in a second mirror on the wall behind us, and behind that yet another double and then another, reproduced each time smaller and smaller until it seems the last of them must be miles away.

I am there to ensure he does not linger too long while my mother waits on the broiling sidewalk outside. It's a mission I've been on before, most often when Sunday dinner is ready and my father has not returned from McGuire's. McGuire's has a black-and-white television on a shelf above the bar, its small screen covered by a sheet of blue plastic. I enter the bar through a screen door at the rear of the building, my eyes gradually adjusting to the gloom. When the bartender spots me he nods meaningfully toward my father. Without taking his eyes off the beer glass in his hand, my father pats the top of the bar stool beside him and tells the bartender to give me a glass of Coca-Cola. I know

I should refuse. But the sun has made me thirsty and I am fascinated by the antics of the tiny figures on the pretend-color TV – my father's beloved baseball Giants. I don't know there is anything else to watch on television until three years later when we get a set of our own. I climb the tall stool with difficulty, and the world behind the bar is revealed to me: the deep well of the walkway where the bartender, the only sober man in the place, moves back and forth amid the leaky beer taps, gray sink water and sparkling glassware.

My father has already consumed several glasses of the amber fluid the bartender draws with a flourish like a midway magician from one of the taps behind the bar, each capped with the colorful logo of its brewer: Schlitz, Pabst Blue Ribbon, Reingold. I know from experience how two hours earlier, fresh from eleven-o'clock mass, my father's then-sober expression has altered Lon Chaney-like as the first sip of beer passed through his gullet, a transformation as grotesque and fascinating as anything in a horror film, his Adam's apple rising and falling like a valve to receive the bitter liquid, the loud swallowing sound he makes palpable with pleasure: Dr. Jekyll turning into Mr. Hyde. His thick lips are moist with anticipation of more to come, his brown-flecked green eyes already under the spell of the subterranean man set free by the mere tincture of alcohol contained in that first sip, far less than a priest consumes during mass without showing any effect, the blood of Christ having less visible consequence than a few ounces of cheap lager.

It is cool and dark in that bar, in all the bars I've been in on similar missions. I like their smell and still inhale deeply every time I pass an old gin mill, the rancid-beer odor that saturates its dark walls and sawdust floor making it impervious to any scrubbing or painting and rendering that particular piece of real estate useless for anything but another of its kind or the wrecking ball. To this day I have little appetite and even less tolerance for alcohol, but the smell of beer is the willy-nilly fragrance of my childhood. It lingers in the thin glass tumbler my father forbids me to use for milk, eye-wateringly pungent in the pool of piss-colored remains at its bottom that I sniff like a mouse and then test disappointingly on my tongue. I much prefer the tart Tom Collinses my mother lets me sip when company comes to visit, her own expression unchanged even by hard liquor, no mystery for me to plumb at the bottom of her tall frosted glass, just a kind of enhanced lemonade and then a lightheadedness that ends in headache and early bedtime. No evil potion, no devil's-brew-on-tap.

I glance toward this bar's one small window that discretely peeps out onto the baking street, but there is no sign of my mother. I feel a giddy contraction of my bowels, the same feeling I get if I think I've become separated from her while forced to endure yet another Macy's white sale or when I think how close Christmas is or when my mother has in fact abandoned me, flying off to her cousin's in the Bronx while I stand balling at the front door, restrained from running after her by my big sister who seems to take an evil pleasure in my anguish. My mother has never entered a bar, not even to retrieve a dallying husband, and there is not much chance she will do so this day.

"Mommy's waiting," I declare to my father's balding skull, its Sitting Bull nose a waxy yellow in the half-light.

He raises the fluted ten-cent-beer glass and drinks, his throat rising and falling with the same precision he brings to the balancing of his checkbook or his toenail-clipping.

"In a minute."

Not spoken in anger or threat, he mouths the words from the corner of his mouth to avoid confronting me, as if I were a disembodied voice that cannot be ignored and will not be appeased despite my half-finished Coca-Cola rapidly turning to ice water. But there is a warning in his tone that will keep me from saying anything more until he is halfway through his next beer.

I feel I should leave him and go back to my mother before she abandons us both. But returning to her without my father means failing to achieve what she has sent me here to do and risk her own anger, or tears. I hate to see my mother cry. She never sheds a false tear, and her weeping is horribly disfiguring. Her high straight nose is all that remains as the rest of her face collapses on itself, her nearsighted gray eyes flooding with misery, her thin lips yanked downward as if an implement of torture is being applied. Until I am a grown man I don't know a woman can weep for anything but deep, tragic reasons.

"In a minute," he says again and waves his empty glass at the bartender who is reading a racing form halfway down the bar. My father and a gray, rumpled man whose gaze has never left the inside of his own glass are the only customers. I never see my father speak to anyone in bars but bartenders, though he is garrulous as a young Labrador every place else, never stopping for a gallon of gasoline without getting out of the car to chat up the station attendant. It's obvious to me that bartenders only talk to him because it's their job. But of course I am not privy to what goes on when he visits these places by himself.

I am sent on other missions of redemption – to church, the purpose of which is also salvation, my own. Both bars and darkened churches are full of the scents that make them what they are: stale beer and whiskey in one, incense and candle wax in the other. Virtue is the object of my mission in both, doing the will of God or my mother, which are really much the same thing. In a few years I will be an altar boy. Already I pretend to say mass on the kitchen table, using teacups and Dugan's spongy white bread for the species. I also give sermons standing on a kitchen chair, imitations of the crazy Irish pastor that amuse my mother who, despite the vale of tears she walks in and the hopes she has for my career in the clergy, loves a laugh.

Sometimes when no altar boy shows up for mass or is more than a few minutes late, my father will rise from the pew where he has been kneeling with his missal open to the day's Introit, approach the altar where the priest has begun making the Latin responses for himself, kneel down beside the priest's white or green or rose-colored chasuble, the letters "IHS" stitched elegantly into its back, and begin the acolyte's responses. The priest doesn't even turn to see who it is who has come forward, as if my father has been sent by God like the "strangers" in the Bible story my mother reads me about Abraham and Sarah who has a baby at the age of ninety even though she has laughed at the angel-messenger's prophecy. Later, after I have myself been accepted into the fraternity of acolytes, I will also come forward to fill in for a missing altar boy like an off-duty cop stopping to direct traffic during an emergency or to foil a robbery in progress. When the boy I am scheduled to serve with does not show up, my father will sometimes join me, though one acolyte can easily handle the Latin responses as well as both servers' duties. My father kneels on the opposite side of the altar steps with never a glance my way, erect in his Sunday suit or, in hot weather, starched white open-neck shirt, his expression full of piety. My *pius Aeneas*.

II

As a child he suffered from such bad headaches his mother had relics applied to his skull. A momma's boy, the darling of a saintly woman who prayed he would one day be ordained a priest, his father died several years before I was born. That man, Anthony, was short, with a big black mustache. In the sepia photos I've seen he stands next to a terrified seated woman who looks very much like my Aunt Francie, one of the few Seifferts I am permitted to know and, so to speak, embrace. Anthony spent as much time away from home as he could, "home" being a wood-frame house on Maple Street in the section of town known as West Fort Lee. My grandfather, whom my father detested, made frequent trips back to what he still considered the old country, though he was born and lived in Manhattan before moving to Fort Lee—mostly on 125th Street back when Harlem was a German enclave, so much so that my father, third-generation American, didn't speak English until he was five.

My father's maternal grandfather, an immigrant from a small town in Bavaria, kept a vegetable garden after the family moved to New Jersey, and throughout his life my father couldn't resist sticking a tomato plant into any unclaimed patch of dirt he came upon. The day we took that bus to 168th Street our back yard was burgeoning with green beans, yellow squash, wax beans, tomatoes, potatoes and even four-foot-high corn, all in a bit of ground no bigger than a modest swimming pool. I ate it all right off the vine and on long summer evenings begged to be allowed to water all that delicious bounty, a privilege I was allowed only under my father's close supervision.

It was his mother who determined the sort of boy, and then man, he would be, though he didn't last much more than a year in the seminary, the priesthood being her fondest hope for him, just as it was my mother's for her own three sons. My father's maternal aunt had produced both a priest and a nun. The nun was a kind of saint whose heart sometimes stopped for no apparent reason and didn't restart for much longer periods of time than her doctors believed it was possible to do and survive. By the time I met her, Cousin Julia was already retired from the convent for medical reasons while still relatively young. I only met her once, but she left a lasting impression because of the very un-nunlike delight she took in "The Poor People of Paris," a popular tune I was very fond of myself.

My mother once told me it was a good thing my father didn't become a priest because he would have been a bad one. I understood her to mean he would have been a bad anything – husband, father, as well as a bad employee to the uncle who hired him out of compassion during the depths of the Depression. I could see for myself the bad brother he was to my Uncle Joe whom he once ejected from our front porch for being "inebriated" – one of the big words he liked to use, though he usually mistook their meanings ("in lieu of" for "in view of,") and prefaced his malaprops with sententious phrases like "speaking in the vernacular," though his intent was to do just the opposite.

One Sunday afternoon I came home from playing with my friend Larry to find Uncle Joe and my mother sitting on our enclosed front porch. I remember the occasion so well partly because Joe, who rarely came by our house and probably was never invited to do so, was in tears and the only other grown man I had seen cry was my father. When sober Joe seemed to me a quiet, gentle man. He worked as a gravedigger for his brother-in-law, Aunt Francie's husband, who was in charge of the parish cemetery. Joe never failed to wave when he saw me on the street and tell me to give his regards to my mother. All he was guilty of that warm afternoon my father found him weeping on our front porch was drunken grief: the woman he loved had dumped him.

Joe must have been in his middle or late thirties at the time, too old to be having girlfriends. But my mother was talking to him in a way I had never heard her talk to my father, a man who required discipline not sympathy. "There's more than one pebble on the beach," she said, "more than one fish in the ocean." Both of these aphorisms were new to me and seemed a startling and enigmatic use of language. There were thousands, even millions of pebbles on a beach. Was it possible there were so many women to choose from, even for a drunk like Joe? And what was it about the sea and its environs that love thwarted and the hope for new love suggested?

This was the scene my father walked into when he returned home from McGuire's tavern. He was right about one thing: Joe was "inebriated," barely able to sit up in the green straight-backed chair which, along with my brother's old desk, were the only furniture in that small screened-in space. The porch was my secular chapel, private parlor and sometimes laboratory. I played endless board games there with friends and sheltered wounded birds until they were strong enough to fly again. I raised two kittens there whom I named Mary and Kitty for my mother and her cousin and best friend in the Bronx, until they destroyed the porch's tall screens and disappeared overnight. When I felt out of sorts I would assume the lotus position on the shelf beneath the top of that green desk until my anxiety passed.

As soon as my father saw the state his brother was in, he ordered him to leave, though he had come home himself every bit as drunk, one time passing out on the staircase between living room and the bedrooms on the second floor, where he spent the rest of the night unnoticed until morning. Joe was in no condition to protest. The younger brother, I could see he stood in fear of my father. He struggled to his feet and somehow made it down the steep brick front stoop and staggered the half block to Main Street and the bus stop outside Kaplan's drugstore. He still lived in West Fort Lee a mile away, so there was no question of his walking home, and on a Sunday afternoon you could wait an hour for the 82 bus to come along. After my parents had gone back in the house I watched him remain upright only by holding onto the pole supporting the bus-stop sign, a round black-and-white silhouette of a young woman placing her shapely calf confidently onto a bus's first step—the same sign that marked bus stops all the way from the George Washington Bridge to the end of the run in Hackensack.

In my memory there is no one else on the street that afternoon and hardly any traffic, just Uncle Joe who was hardly an uncle at all because he had no status in our house or my life, one of the shadowy Seifferts, the bad seed from Maple Street. When the bus finally arrived, it slowed down as if to stop, but when the driver saw the condition Joe was in, he accelerated and left my uncle reeling in its wake. I have often wondered how Uncle Joe got home that day.

I understood why my father was a bad husband and a bad father: You didn't come home drunk the way he did if you were a caring spouse, and you didn't behave that way if you were a good father. Bad employee had to be explained to me many years later, because he did get up and go to work each morning no matter in what condition he was in the previous night. One of the family legends was how the morning after a blizzard he wrapped his legs in newspapers and walked across the George Washington Bridge into Manhattan because the buses were not running and the bridge was closed anyway to vehicular traffic.

Early on I recognized my father was a lower form of human life than other men, certainly a lower form than my mother. By association, his entire family also were lesser beings, not just morally inferior but sub-par in every way—innately and incorrigibly lacking in judgment, intelligence, trustworthiness, table manners and even physical appearance. His hooked nose was an eyesore, his thick lips a sign of base sensuality, his white hairless legs an embarrassment on public beaches. And all of this was inextricably tied to his being German. Never mind that he was three times removed from the immigrant, that he bore no responsibility for the Nazi death camps, that he didn't even know what part of Germany he came from until my oldest brother tracked down that side of the family after *Roots* inspired a generation of Americans to dig up their long-buried and probably best-left-alone ancestors. In our house German meant bad, just as Irish meant good.

No racist ideas have ever gone further in simplistically categorizing human beings as the one I accepted from an early age about my parents lineage. "Irish" and "German" were as absolute as "white" and "black" were in the world beyond my own (a place still very much removed from the great metropolis across the river—we rarely saw an African American pass through Fort Lee, never mind lived near one). This was Manicheanism of a very basic variety, light and dark, good and evil, male and female. Needless to say, German-male-bad versus Irish-female-good translated into my own emerging identity in the years to come with formidable consequences.

When my father was nine years the Austro-Hungarian Empire along with its German allies began a mutual blood bath with their British, French and Russian cousins that would radically change the face of Europe, the world itself and a young boy's idea of what it meant to be German American. One of his earlier memories was of a poster depicting a German soldier hoisting the body of a young baby on the end of his bayonet. During those war years the American government openly spied on, imprisoned and even lynched Germans and US citizens of German descent—ordinary people going about their business making a living and raising a family. To be German no longer meant being the heir of a high European culture, the center of scholarship, music and philosophy, its universities educating not just its own brilliant students but the world's best and brightest. Being German suddenly came to mean automatic suspicion, in possible league with the monsters who slaughtered babies and raped Belgian nuns—all the propaganda that made the reports about what was actually happening to Jews during the next world war too fantastic to believe for those who remembered how they were gulled twenty years earlier.

But my father didn't give much conscious thought to these matters when he was still twelve years old, delivering groceries up and down the hills of West Fort Lee out of a second-hand wagon, his dog Prince trotting along at his side. His thoughts were on the pleasures of golf and, to a lesser extent, his future career in the priesthood. Fort Lee was an avid baseball town, but there was a private golf course abutting the cemetery behind the parish church perched upon the western edge of the narrow plateau atop the Hudson Palisades. The terrain fell off sharply from there, making for spectacular sunsets, especially during Saturday May processions Catholic schoolchildren were required to attend. The steep drop also made for technical problems both for my Uncle Frank who was responsible for maintaining the cemetery grave sites, as well as for the owners of that golf course.

My father discovered golf soon after he first started to frequent the old—old even in his own childhood—parish church, a brownstone English-style chapel that could hold no more than a couple hundred people. Even in his childhood there were more than that many Catholics in Fort Lee, so there had to be multiple masses on Sunday to accommodate them. As an altar boy he was required to serve at least one of those masses, sometimes more, as well as to be available for weekend weddings. He was also taken out of class to serve midweek funerals. The cemetery afforded an excellent view of the sixth and ninth fairways of the golf course, a detail that caught my father's attention when he was standing next to an open grave holding a censer and bucket of holy water. On bright spring and autumn mornings the course's lush green fairways and undulating greens were bathed in sunlight, with twosomes putting out and foursomes just teeing off.

The golf course became a source of income as he grew older and could offer his services as a caddy. He learned the game by watching the better golfers and by picking up pointers from the course pro who didn't mind having a youngster like my father hanging about, a boy with natural ability for the game. By the time my father was fifteen and looking for his first job in New York, he was scoring in the low eighties and had dreams of being sponsored by some rich old duffer so he could enter something more ambitious than the local tournaments where he was already winning or placing second or third, competing against much older boys and even young men. It was golf he missed most when he was away that year at seminary. Not girls, not his mother's cooking. His longing for green fairways even became a point of discussion with his confessor who told him the devil was using golf as a lure to pry him away from his vocation. Perhaps if my father had chosen a less ascetic order than the Carmelites or had entered the diocesan seminary in his home state instead of distant Chicago, he would not have felt such a keen sense of loss. It was not unheard of, after all, for a parish curate to play a round now and then, something no Carmelite did in those days.

On the other hand, it wasn't just the bright sunlight on the lush fairways or the fragrance of freshly watered greens that took such a firm grip on his young imagination. Even when he was still just a caddy he had glimpsed the easy life inside the club house, especially on weekends when members brought their wives to have dinner and dance the new jazz music to a hired orchestra. This was a life he had never imagined, had only witnessed in silent movies, many of which were made right there in Fort lee, the original Hollywood. He also heard stories how movie actors and actresses carried on in the taverns of nearby Coytesville. Like most other young men he had been ordered to stay away from that part of town, especially at night. But he had learned about Theta Barra's antics in a tank of water with nothing on but a skin-tight bathing suit, of drunken parties that went on until it was time for the revelers to be back on the set for the day's shooting. Some of those movie stars played golf on the same course where my father caddied. He once carried the clubs of a young John Barrymore and was given a five-dollar tip for his effort, an unheard of amount of money that he promptly turned over to his mother.

"Who gave you this?" she demanded in her heavy Brooklyn accent, assuming no one would part with that kind of money for merely being helped to play a game. She recognized the actor's name, though she had never gone to a movie herself and had no idea of the man's reputation on and off the screen as a lovable reprobate. "If he asks you to do anything funny, you tell him no, you understand?"

"Yes, mom," my father said, not having the slightest idea what sort of "funny" thing such a man could ask of him. Probably his mother didn't either, certainly not the kind of "funny" things that boys got thrown out of seminary for doing with other boys or grown men got put into jail for doing with other men. It was just that his mother's command of the English language, despite being American-born, was as hobbled as his own by the disability of not having learned it until she was almost school age. Words like "funny" had to serve a multitude of purposes, leaving her son to divine what she was really talking about, just as later on I had to construe as best I could what my father meant when he turned red and referred to "you-know-what."

All things considered, between the lure of the links and Theta Barra's aquatics, the odds were heavily against heaven and much in favor of the devil. Only a natural or God-made eunuch could have remained untouched by those twin sirens, not to mention the lure of the great city across the Hudson just a ferry ride away. By the time my mother met him in a bank on Wall Street where they both were working as tellers at the respective ages of twenty and seventeen, he was so dark from playing golf that, with his hook nose and jet black hair, she took him for Italian.

III

She was a slim, spirited child. In photographs she looks as skinny as her younger sister Nora who stands beside her like a phantom, there and not there, dead just short of her eleventh birthday. My mother never got over Nora's death. It was the informing tragedy of her youth and conditioned much of her attitudes and habits for the rest of her life. All mothers in my day cautioned their children against putting their mouths on public drinking fountains and otherwise exposing themselves to germs. But for me the consequences of contagion were fatally embodied in that thin girl in the photograph who seems to resemble her so much—unlike her other, surviving sister who was so dissimilar to my mother both in looks and personality.

When I was newly married I invited my parents to dinner at the brownstone apartment in Brooklyn where I had recently moved with my new wife and child. When my mother saw I lived just a few blocks from Buttermilk Channel, the narrow strip of water that separates Brooklyn from Governor's Island, she asked why I had chosen to live in such a depressing neighborhood. It turned out her sister Nora had died of Typhus on Governor's Island in a public hospital, a horrible place, little more than a warehouse for the terminally ill. My mother been to visit her there and watched her waste away.

Three years before she met my father she passed the entrance exam for Cathedral High School, but there was no money for tuition so she remained at home to take care of her younger brothers until she was of age to get a paying job. Both her parents were immigrants from County Kerry, neither of them educated beyond the ability to read and write. Her mother had eight children, counting Nora. Her father bounced from job to job—trolley-car conductor, building superintendent, gin-mill proprietor. The family moved with him from one job to the next, especially during his superintendent days. Getting a real job of her own was a liberation for my mother, an end to the incessant diaper-changing and house chores, entry into the adult world of subway trains and lunch hours—and of course romance.

The latter came in the form of my father, though not before there had been a few flirtations, a Jewish fellow in particular—throughout her life she always spoke fondly of Jews—bright, good-looking, who recognized in my mother someone like himself, keen for the finer things of life and equipped with the abilities to enjoy them. But she ended up with my father, cocky, dark, owner of a new motor car, a commuter from the other side of the river where the real Americans lived, a people she had only seen in silent movies, most of them made just a few blocks from where my father grew up and which gave him his own idea of what the good life was. They each saw in the other their individual ambitions personified: for my father, a beautiful high-spirited girl unsullied but ready for the post-war orgy of alcohol and freedom that we call the Roaring Twenties. In him she saw something exotic, self-assured and indigenous in a way she would never feel herself to be, and with a bank account and good prospects to boot. She also saw a way out of not just the drudgery of standing all day in a teller's cage but liberation from the cooking and cleaning that were still her lot when she returned home at the end of her working day. "Little did I realize," she would tell me, "I was jumping out of the frying pan and into the fire."

She stands now stoical as a nun in her Sunday best on the hot sidewalk outside that gin mill on upper Broadway, waiting for her husband to finish his beer. Almost twenty years have passed since they first glimpsed each other across the gray Formica tables of the Horn & Hardart Automat on Vesey Street, each of them having opted for the five-cent baked-bean special. Twenty years and four children, two years of the good life in an apartment on upper Fifth Avenue, her husband riding high with a great future in Chemical Corn Exchange while keeping books on the side for a few speakeasies, then the birth of their first child followed closely by the collapse of the stock market on which her husband's present job and her future security depended. Within a year they had another child and were reduced to living with her mother's family in the Bronx. A few years after that she found herself exiled to New Jersey, where would mourn her fate like an ancient Hebrew in Babylon, longing for the Zion of her youth across the Hudson.

She thinks to herself, she might as well have stayed home and baked yet another Sunday pot roast. It had been the lure of spending an afternoon in the City, even if it was going to be someplace in Queens, a county she had never been to, that brought her to this pass. Any part of New York City had to be better than the prospect of yet another week with nothing but more washing and ironing to look forward to. We are supposed to meet up with a co-worker of her husband, or someone he met through his job, she isn't sure which and doesn't much care. My father is always bringing home one of these so-called friends or, more properly, they are bringing him home, since they inevitably are in better shape than he is when they arrive. Her husband has no real friends, no one to spend his free time with instead of hanging out in McGuire's. He doesn't seem to want any. But every so often he attaches himself to one of these strays, men whose wives have walked out on them or who have never married. He will call ahead—if two minutes before she is ready to put the food on the table is "ahead"—that she should make a place for one more. Then there is the long wait after she has fed the children, but not herself, until he and his new acquaintance show up.

The worst of it is, she can't find anything to criticize about those men. They are inevitably well-mannered, reasonably sober and sincerely grateful for the food she puts in front of them. They are also good conversationalists when my father gives them the chance to get a word in edgewise, which isn't until he has passed out on the couch and she has the friend to herself, a mixed blessing because it is awkward trying to carry on a conversation with a stranger while your husband lies in a drunken stupor a few feet away like a man at his own wake. The experience inevitably fills her with conflicting feelings, some of which she dares not recognize. When her guest leaves she feels both relief and abandonment, especially if he is a New Yorker himself and has talked about the City and the ways it has changed since she lived there. With the stranger gone and her husband unconscious, she has the rest of the evening to herself. All she need do is remove my father's shoes and throw a blanket over him. Then she can abandon herself to one of her novels or listen to the radio or just sit and brood.

It never occurs to her to analyze what it is in her husband's personality that draws him to these men in the first place. She can sense the longing in him for male companionship and relates it to his father's abandonment of him and his brothers and sisters. But, why does he seek out friendship only when he is three sheets to the wind? Why not when he is sober and able to forge a real relationship like other men? She feels bad that she can't satisfy this longing in him for companionship, but her feeling never amounts to anything as strong as sympathy, the hurt he causes by his behavior making it turn to resentment before it has a chance to become something more benevolent. "Whatever became of So-and-So?" she asks a week or two after he has brought home one of his one-night buddies. She only puts this question to him when he is sober and, to give him his due, mostly he is sober. "Why don't you have him come by again? He seemed like a nice enough fellow." To which my father responds with a dismissive wave of his hand and a guttural noise. But a month later when he is in his cups again he befriends some other loner, or chats up the TV repairman until the fellow is only too glad to get away—even at the age of five or six I can see that.

The only place he finds any lasting bond is with his cousin, the priest and brother of the almost-saint, and with my mother's brothers. It is for this reason that my maternal uncles are effectively banned from our house. They are all hard drinkers, even Tom and Rodie who never joined the police force. But it seems obvious to my mother that they

tolerate rather than enjoy her husband's company, as if he were a kind
of mascot rather than an equal. They despise their other brother-in-law,
an immigrant from Ireland, a highly opinionated man who, despite
being physically small, stands up to them at wakes and weddings when
they insult him. Sometimes it ends in a fight, and of course the
brother-in-law loses, but he never allows them to abuse him without
defending his honor. By contrast, those men pay little attention to my
father and his opinions, to the extent he has any, perhaps because he
admires them so much and even tries to emulate them.

She can feel the hot concrete through the soles of her
medium-heeled oxfords. Traffic is light heading on Broadway. There are
few pedestrians on the street and just a few buses parked in the open-air
terminal next to the bar where my father is nursing yet another beer. All
the routes to and from New Jersey begin and end their runs here. The
82 that refused to pick up Uncle Joe started its route here, following
Main Street through Fort Lee until it turns into Fort Lee Road when
it leaves the town proper and heads through what we euphemistically
call the Meadows, the great smelly swamp in the low land behind and
below the Hudson Palisades—the same route George Washington's
army took when the British surprised them at their dinner almost two
hundred years earlier.

For my mother that route, both westward and eastward into the
City, is a lifeline, her only connection with a life beyond Fort Lee, a
burg of no more than two thousand souls until the second world war.
The movie industry has long since deserted the town for the sunnier
climes of California. Only one film processing plant remains of what
once was Fort Lee's main economic engine during the silent-film era.
My best friend's maiden aunt still works there as a cutter, a woman
who can remember when movies provided work for virtually every
able-bodied male or female who wanted it whether in the industry
itself or as a lifeguard, waiter or housekeeper for the big resort that
stood on the Hudson River just north of where the bridge was later

built, or at one of the nightclubs atop the Palisades. A godly woman who rarely goes to movies and keeps to herself in the single room she rents in her married brother's house, she sometimes faints at what she sees projected onto the cutting room screen—Jane Russell's big breasts spilling into the camera lens or worse. It is an odd job for a woman of her virginal sensibility, but the fact that she still holds such a position, a relatively lucrative one, is indication of what movies used to mean to the town.

But for my mother, a transplant, and one that will never take root or at least will not do so until many decades have passed when she begins to feel as uncomfortable with what New York has become as native Fort Leeites did back when she first arrived there, the 82, the only route convenient to the house on Center Avenue we occupied for those few short years during and after the second world war, is her escape hatch into the bustling familiarity of Manhattan or the still fantasyland of the Fox and Oritani theaters in Hackensack. There is a clock to the right of the big screen in the Fox, its numbers glowing phosphorescent blue beside the giant images of Robert Taylor and Claudette Colbert. My mother stays until the minute hand reaches a critical point, sometime between four and five p.m., then rushes us out to catch the 82 back to Fort Lee in time to put on her husband's supper. Meanwhile she loses herself in those images on the screen, forgets she is an exile in a strange land where even the Roman Catholic religion means something different from what it did in her youth, something restrictive and puritanical, the joyless faith of a people whose only pleasure in life seems to come out of a beer tap.

There's a sepia wedding photo taken in 1928 on my parents' honeymoon in Atlantic City, a formal shot with my mother seated, as in those wedding portraits of previous generations, beside the standing figure of her new husband. But my mother's dress ends several inches above her knees and her own mother certainly never allowed herself the kind of smile captured in that photograph, probably not even in her bedroom. My father's expression is a bit dazed, as if what has just happened to him is eminently satisfying though still a bit beyond his wildest hopes. It's a picture of two young people full of the confidence that only the first flush of adulthood can enjoy. There is no hint in it of the sobering Crash that will plunge them twenty-two months later into a life of penny-pinching bickering and, for her husband, hard drinking of a sort my mother never witnessed among her father and brothers at their worst. Until her marriage she has never known a man who could not hold his liquor, who passes out in the middle of a party and spends long hours retching his guts out afterward. For years she believes my father when he tells her he has a bad stomach; otherwise why don't the men of her own family react the same way to alcohol?

That honeymoon photo is huge, almost poster-size. As a child, I am as impressed by its girth as I am by that dress and smile. It might be an old movie poster, "The Follies of '28." The woman is certainly beautiful enough for the part—how did that generation manage to turn out so many stunning women? By the time I first see that photo my mother is almost forty and my father has lost most of his hair. The woman I know wears calf-length house dresses, sensible shoes and keeps her hair pinned on top of her head, a matronly figure who doesn't like to have her picture taken and doesn't smile much. She also wears glasses, all the time, blue plastic frames that are anything but attractive. She might be an older sister or aunt to the young woman with the bare thighs in that wedding photo. She certainly can't be the woman herself.

On the wall behind my desk is another picture, the one I've used as model for the two people I described in the previous paragraph—a tight-lipped woman kneeling on the thin lawn of our back yard on Center Avenue and a balding man squatting a few feet away. Between them is a child, me, an arm around each of their necks, their missing link, perhaps the strongest if not the only tie that still binds them together. By today's standards they both seem older than their years. There is some sort of pendant lying on the breast of the white dress my mother has put on for the occasion—most likely a piece of jewelry; she would have worn her Miraculous Medal privately, underneath her clothes. She is staring intently at the camera minus the eyeglasses without which she can see very little, the expression on her face the suspicious scowl of the semi-blind, something between a smile, annoyance and trepidation, the look of an aborigine who believes a camera can steal her soul. In the photo my father seems physically slighter than her. In fact, he stood five inches taller, but his arms and legs are very thin, though he spends most of his free time repairing and adding to our house. His hair, however much it has already receded, is carefully combed, and the shoes he is wearing are the brown-and-white oxfords I also own a pair of. He has on a long-sleeve dress shirt rolled up to the elbows and light-colored slacks.

My head seems large in the photo, way out of proportion to the rest of my young body. I'm wearing worn, baggy short pants, my "play clothes," held up by suspenders over a clean white short-sleeve shirt. My legs are as spindly as those of a child in a newsreel about some famine-stricken part of the world. I am frequently sick, sometimes seriously. But my smile is wide, not so much the innocent grin of a child as the cocky grin of one of the boys at a beery reunion hanging onto the necks of his old school chums or hunting mates. My father's smile by comparison is subdued but full of conceit. He believes himself to be a good-looking man, a man worth photographing, and spends an inordinate amount of time in front of the bathroom mirror carefully parting his thin black hair.

The wall of my study near this photo is covered with photos of my own children as well as an enlargement of a portrait of my father, a picture taken for his employer's in-house newsletter when he was named employee of the month. He's about the same age in the photo as I am now, late fifties. There is the same self-confidence that is evident in the earlier snapshot, though now of a more relaxed, less arrogant variety—he was a teetotaler by this time compared with his earlier self—and of course he is dressed in a dark business suit. His hair is gray for a couple inches above each ear and then, though still dark, only visible at the crown of his head. This was his work persona, the man he became when he left our house each morning to earn our bread when there was no conflict in him and he knew exactly who he was and what he was about.

My mother knows both men, the beery rake and the responsible breadwinner. But the most she admits to knowing of the latter is a rare backhand compliment. "There is good in your father as well." Protecting this good but fragile side of him from the Evil One is her full-time job.

In the first heady days of their marriage when they lived on upper Fifth Avenue in a building with a doorman and all sorts of crooked politicians and theater people for neighbors, all that seemed required of as a wife was to hold his head when he was expelling the excess booze he consumed in the speakeasies where he worked on the side as a bookkeeper. She was proud of his industry and took it for granted that, given the opportunity, men would drink, though she wasn't used to their getting sick as a result. "If you don't have the stomach for it, why don't you leave it alone?" she asked when he was more sober but still wretched. Sometimes he blamed his nausea and headache not on his own excess or his stomach but on bad alcohol. He was lucky, he said, he didn't go blind from it.

After Prohibition ended there could be no more excuses of bad booze, and that was when he came up with a bad stomach. During their courting days he had been hospitalized with what turned out to be appendicitis. My mother was not clear about the distinction between the appendix and the intestines, so she accepted this explanation as well, though the cure for his illness still seemed to her to be abstinence or at least some measure of moderation. She drank herself in those days, but not to the point of inebriation, and certainly not to the point that she became physically ill. It was a long time before she came to see that alcohol wasn't so much the problem for her husband as the expression of it. But what the problem actually was escaped her, and always would. The man was an enigma, a stranger in her midst. There was very little in her experience of her Irish and Irish-American relatives that prepared her for dealing with a John Seiffert. His foreign looks but genuine American upbringing came to seem incidental by comparison with the powerful demons that possessed him.

Apart from the appearance of familial harmony in that snapshot—by the short shadows it appears to have been taken in the middle of a summer's day—the picture is deceptive for the very reason that the house and yard, the only property we ever owned in my childhood or adolescence, in just a few years would no longer be ours.

"Home" is ultimately a memory, the place where your spirit seemed happiest for however brief a time. A fetid tenement, a summer house, a jail cell, even a grave, it has to occupy a physical site, but what it finally amounts to is so much more than turf and bricks and two-by-fours. It's the smell of lilacs that run riot in early May, not just filling the neighborhood but every room in the house with their sweet, almost unbearably sweet smell. It's sunlight slanting across a wretched lawn and luxuriant vegetable garden at seven o'clock of a June evening; the hiss of a hose as its spray sends arcing rainbows over the corn and tomato plants. It's your older brother throwing open the bedroom window on an exquisitely blue October morning; the sounds of rain gently hammering on the roof of a front porch; the smells that come out of damp wood and paint when the air is so humid the wood would sweat if it could. Home is where that part of you goes on living long after you have moved elsewhere and grown old. It tugs at you and is perhaps better left unrevisited, because no matter how much bad there was connected with it, it always remains a paradise lost, the one time in your existence when life was complete, when all the characters that should be there were there, when happiness seemed not only possible but a daily routine that could so easily be mistaken for normalcy.

MARY
IV

My name is Mary Teresa Veronica O'Connor Seiffert. I was born February 11th, 1909. My parents were Irish immigrants from County Kerry. They had eight children. One of them, Nora, died at the age of ten. I attended P.S. 69 in New York City but never got the chance to go to high school, though I was accepted by Cathedral, the diocesan school in Manhattan. On January 6th, 1928 I married John Seiffert from Fort Lee, New Jersey. I've given birth to five children, four boys and a girl. I had to have a special operation so I could have Tommy, the fourth. The fifth child was born in 1952, whom I named Steven, after the first martyr. But he was badly deformed and only lived a few hours.

That's pretty much the story of my life in a nutshell. I did what I had to do, accepting God's will as best I could and with a cheerful grace whenever possible. I won't say it's been easy, but there are plenty that have had it worse, the Jews in Germany, for instance, or the blacks in Africa. I did what I could to help them, and still do, but God knows I haven't been a rich woman.

I'm old now and I've been told I have old-timer's disease or whatever it's called, so my memory's starting to go. I already confuse Tommy with his brothers Jack and Donald when I talk to him on the phone. Some days I can't remember what one or the other of my children looks like without checking the photos inside the hutch in my tiny living room. I'm not so far gone I can't still manage on my own, and my oldest lives just a couple miles away and stops by most afternoons for a cup of tea. But it's just a matter of time, so if I'm going to put anything down on paper while I still have my wits about me I'd better do it now.

I'm writing this, actually, for their sake, for my children, to set the record straight. There's been a lot of confusion over the years, especially when John was still alive, why I did one thing or another. There's been a lot of resentment and bad blood. I didn't mean anyone harm. I love all my children. But it's struck me an explanation might help them understand why I acted the way I did.

I was eighteen years old when I married. That wasn't so young in those days, but looking back I realize I wasn't ready for marriage. I'm not trying to make excuses, but when I see how young women nowadays wait till they're twenty-five or thirty, it strikes me how young eighteen actually is to begin taking on the responsibilities of raising a family. And, of course, that was what marriage meant for someone like myself, an Irish Catholic. You got married and you had children. I never even thought about practicing rhythm until well into the 1930s when my doctor told me I might lose my life if I had another. Even then, I had to get permission from a priest. Nowadays women, even Catholic women, do as they please.

Even so, Jack wasn't born until eighteen months after I got married. Girls matured later in those days than they do now. It wasn't uncommon not to get your period until you were seventeen. I started to get mine at sixteen, but I probably wasn't fully fertile for a couple more years. You'd be surprised how many girls did not have to get married despite what they and their boyfriends got up to simply because they hadn't matured yet. I suppose you could say it was a natural form of birth control.

At first I didn't mind having a child to look after, though I spent most of my youth caring for my brothers, especially the youngest who was born just five years before my Jack. You feel different when a child is your own. You don't mind the shitty diapers so much or getting up in the middle of the night to feed him, and I breast-fed all my children. A baby didn't make me feel like I was any less independent, because it was my own child and my husband and I were living in our own apartment. For a young woman of eighteen, especially one who has never lived on her own the way women commonly do today, that can be a pretty heady experience.

Rita was born eleven months later, so it was almost like having twins from that point on. Even so, for the first year John made a good living and we had a nice apartment on Fifth Avenue. I took Jack out to the park right across the street every afternoon. I loved to walk, I still do but I can't do it like I used to. I used to push him all over Central Park, from one end to the other and over to the West Side. Of course, I'd be scared to death to enter that park now, even in the daytime. Back then I never gave it a second thought. I didn't socialize much with other young mothers. They didn't seem all that eager to socialize with me either, and I was content with my own company and my child's. I was happy, although it was a fool's sort of happiness, because all that while John was carrying on, spending our money in speakeasies and God knows where else. Most nights he came home three sheets to the wind. But I was used to men drinking and didn't think much of it at the time, only it got lonely in that big apartment after the kids were in bed for the night and John was sleeping off his latest boozing.

After the Stock Market crash we had to give up the apartment and move in with my family in the Bronx. For me it was like being sent back to prison. Not only did I have to take up where I left off looking after my youngest brother and helping with the housework, I had two of my own kids into the bargain. To top it off, John had ready-made drinking partners in my brothers. He spent more time with them than he did looking for work, not that there was much work to be found. When he was offered a job with the sanitation department in Fort Lee, I told him he either took it or I would leave him. Of course I wouldn't have done so. A vow is a vow. But I said I would with so much conviction he believed me.

That turned out to be the worst decision of my life. I thought we would move to New Jersey for a while, a year or two, and then we would come back to Manhattan as soon as the depression, or "panic" as they were calling it, was over. Little did I know I would spend virtually the rest of my life in that godforsaken state.

We moved in with John's family on Maple Street. His father had died the previous year, and his funeral was the first time I had to deal with all his family at one time. Did I mention that none of them had attended my wedding? It seemed I wasn't good enough for their son, an Irish girl from the Bronx without a pot to pee in. Imagine what it was like for me to have to live in the same house with them after that. His mother, Julia, wasn't so bad, but his sister Barbara was a hellion with a set of lungs you could hear six blocks away. As the eldest girl she and John waged a perpetual war for precedence. John moved me there with two children still at the breast and expected me to fend for myself. Somehow I did, and even ended up nursing his mother through her final illness, though none of her children ever gave me credit for it. To them I was and always remained a fast New York girl who had just about kidnapped their darling Johnny.

If I hadn't been so young and hadn't known any better, I never would have survived those couple years. Nothing I did was right. When I sat on my husband's lap, something he used to delight in when we lived by ourselves, he told me not to because his mother and sisters were scandalized. And I thought he must be right. It was only later the anger came, when I realized how cheaply he let me be treated instead of standing up for his wife as any self-respecting man would. He was a mama's boy, and despite the battle royals he waged with Barbara, his sisters both looked on him as the apple of their eyes, and the younger brothers lived in fear of him, especially after their father's death when he started to consider himself head of the clan.

The house on Maple Street was a big wood-frame affair about half a mile from the parish church. Almost as soon as me and my children set foot inside the door I was given to understand I would be expected to attend not just Sunday mass, which of course I did anyway, but other church services too, such as Expositions of the Blessed Sacrament and novenas. My family have been Roman Catholic since Adam, but I never experienced this sort of Catholicism before. My brothers attended mass on Sunday when they weren't too hung over, and managed to drag themselves to confession once a year to make their Easter Duty, but that was about it. My mother never missed mass but neither did she feel obligated to go to church for any other purpose than confession. She even spoke critically of the clergy when they poked their noses into what she considered was none of their affair—politics, for instance. I heard stories from her about priests in Ireland who risked death to say mass for their congregations when the English had forbidden it, "hedgerow priests" she called them because they celebrated mass behind the hedges alongside the fields. But she praised those men not because they were priests but because they defied the British, who my mother hated. She taught her children to hate them too, because of the Famine and all the other dirty business the English got up to with the Irish.

But the Seifferts practiced a different sort of Catholicism. They accepted every word from the mouth of a priest, any priest, as gospel. This seems ironic to me now because the priests in that parish were Irish themselves. In the forty years I lived in that town I don't think Madonna parish ever had a curate who didn't have an Irish last name. The pastor was an immigrant from Tipperary. Even so, my husband's family never once spoke disparagingly of those men, although my own Irishness seemed to be reason to treat me like dirt. Go figure.

John was great for jumping whenever the priests told him to jump, but that didn't stop him from continuing with the same life he had been leading when we lived in New York. His drinking partners changed was all. Half the time I wouldn't see him except for the few hours he spent asleep before he got up to go to that job as a garbage man, thanks to his family's connections. The rest of the time he spent in a gin mill on Main Street whose name I've forgotten—not McGuire's, McGuire's came later when we lived at the other end of town. Some nights he didn't come home at all. He said he stayed at a "friend's" house. I can see now that he brought me back to Fort Lee the way you might bring a pet home, the way he actually did bring home dogs and cats and leave them for me to look after. Once he had me stuck in that house on Maple Street he could go on living his life just the way he did before he got married. I suppose he thought it was his mother's job to look after me. Of course, his mother never said a word against him, at least not in my presence, though she did admit now and then she had maybe pampered him when he was a boy because she expected him to become a priest.

She, Julia, was a small, delicate woman, remarkably soft-spoken in that family of leather-lungs. She was born and raised in the City, so at least we had that much in common. For a while after her marriage she lived on 125th Street, which by the time I married John was a solidly black, or as we said then "Negro," neighborhood. It was she who told me her elder children, John and Barbara, didn't speak English until they were five and starting kindergarten. It seemed incredible to me that an American family whose parents were born and bred in this country could have children who didn't speak English until they were old enough to go to school. But my mother-in-law said that wasn't uncommon among German families, that they were proud of their German heritage back then. That changed, she said, with the first world war.

I enjoyed talking with her because she told me what it was like to be a girl and then a wife and mother back before the turn of the century, what it was like, in other words, in the days when my own mother came to this country and began raising a family. Julia was a kind of exile herself, though I wouldn't say it was the City she felt exiled from. Rather, she seemed out of place in the midst of her own family, and not just because she was quiet and they were loud. It was she, not their gallivanting father, who gave them their religion. She was the one who insisted on their attending church services two or three times a week. Later I found out her brothers and sisters were just as religious as she was. Her sister Anna—we called her "Aunt Annie"—produced both a priest and a nun, and it was Julia's ambition to do the same, though I'd say that apart from John and his younger sister Francie she had slim pickings to work with. I'd never known anyone as religious as she was, and looking back I guess you could say Julia was the reason I became a stronger Catholic myself, partly as a bulwark against John's carryings-on but also because the church became a solace for me and a refuge, especially since it was run by Irish.

Julia had married a ne'er-do-well, and that explained where John got it from. Her family, the Schwartzes, were from Brooklyn. She met her future husband at one of those big beer gardens that used to do a thriving business before the first war, not just in Bushwick but in Manhattan's Yorkville district as well. They weren't so much bars of the kind John and my brothers frequented but big halls and outdoor places where entire families went on Sunday afternoons to eat and drink and dance to oompah music. Anthony Seiffert turned up one afternoon at one of those affairs and introduced himself—he wasn't the shy type, Julia assured me. He was good-looking, dark hair and big black mustache, not very tall but not lacking in confidence on that account. He seemed like the heighth of sophistication to Julia who had only been into Manhattan on two occasions in her eighteen years. He said he had a big job at one of the breweries on 125th Street, which turned out to be only partially true. He worked in a brewery all right, but as a common laborer. She fell for him, and the rest is history, as they say.

The Seifferts were as different from the Schwartzes as my own family was from my husband's. The Seifferts were more interested in having a good time than in saving their souls, while the Schwartzes still practiced the ways of the old country. My husband's father traveled back and forth to Germany almost as frequently as people travel to Europe nowadays, though back then you had to spend a week or more on a ship to do so, and it wasn't cheap either. But he went to the cities of the north, not to Bavaria where his people came from. He considered himself as much German as American, but a sophisticated German, not a country bumpkin like the Schwartzes. He continued to visit Germany even after his marriage, though Julia never felt any desire to go with him and probably wasn't asked. After the family moved to Fort Lee in the early 1900s what she longed for was Brooklyn where she had grown up and been happy.

There was still a lot of German spoken in that house. At first I didn't mind. It reminded me of the Yiddish I had heard in New York and, like the Jews, they didn't so much speak it as use it to leaven their speech, as if an English equivalent couldn't adequately express their meaning. Of course, to the grandfather, Julia's father, they spoke more German than English, but that seemed natural because he was an immigrant. It was only gradually I realized there was none of the humor and playfulness in them I had seen in the Jews in New York. For all their Christianity they were a morose bunch, with the exception of the second daughter Francie who always maintained a cheerful attitude and does so to this day, even after her only son, a cop, was killed in the line of duty and she became widowed a few years later. Like her aunt Annie, Francie produced a nun and almost a priest as well, but the boy became that policeman instead. The daughter left the convent after her brother's death so she could be a comfort to her mother. She then married and had six or seven children, I lost count.

V

"He says, 'Just one more,'" I tell my mother when I exit the bar into the blinding midday light, thinking I am bringing good news because I take everyone's words literally, even though they usually don't mean them that way. She purses her lips tightly and stares through her thick lenses at the opposite side of Broadway, and I know I have failed her. "Expect nothing and you won't be disappointed," is her favorite saying, though like most people who pretend to live by such maxims, she does so mostly in the breach.

"I'll tell him you said hurry up," I stammer and dart back into the bar, more to get away from her anger than in hope of hurrying my father along. From an early age I have sensed she identifies me with my father's sex and thus with that sex's deficiencies. Sending me to a seminary would partly be a way of saving me from myself, from my sex, even if it means the unsexing of me, or *because* it means the unsexing of me, though she certainly never intends anything more insidious by my consecration than a farmer does when he gelds a young stallion so the beast can realize its proper destiny as a servant of humankind undistracted by selfish reproductive urges. When I decide against a career in the clergy my emasculation will not be undone, but her interest in me will diminish. She will not be less of a mother, but since she will no longer be the mother of a priest-to-be, one of the chosen of the Almighty, she will no longer see her role as more than a duty, though still one she will be willing to meet to the full.

Producing a priest would have meant a big step up in her status, not in the social sense but in the pecking order of Creation as she understood it. A priest belonged to a supernatural club, the holy order of Melchesedech, well above any doctor or lawyer or head of state. Generations of dirt-farming Irish women had passed down to her the one ambition any mother, no matter how poor, could aspire to: priest's mother. Such women began and ended their days on their knees praying that God would touch their child with a "vocation," a word that signified an intervention by Jesus Christ into the lives of ordinary mortals no less direct than when he appeared to Saint Margaret Mary as the Sacred Heart or when his own mother visited the children at Fatima. A priest was the next best thing to a clone of the Savior, and no Irish woman misunderstood what that fact implied for herself. Nothing in the secular order stood above the priesthood because it straddled both levels of existence, natural and supernatural. As such, you could not aspire to it, you could only pray you would be called. Hence "vocation," a Latinism and therefore more appropriate than its English equivalent — "calling" — back in the days when the mass and all other church rituals were conducted in what was believed to be the language of heaven, if not of God himself. A woman like my mother, intelligent enough to read Frank Sheed's popularizations of Thomistic philosophy, a woman who once tried to explain to me how the Third Person of the Blessed Trinity was the product of the love generated between the First and Second persons of that Trinity, had never come across any human aspiration or activity that compared with that of being a Roman Catholic priest. What a happy thought for such a woman that the finest and most noble endeavor mankind had ever aspired to was the very one that was open to her sons. And what a disappointment for her to fail to achieve that goal, especially when the signs had seemed so propitious.

She had already failed with my eldest brother who had gone away to a Maryknoll seminary in Ohio at the age of fourteen but returned home after the first year. The next in line, nine years older than myself, had already confided to me he was thinking of becoming a missionary. The two of us sometimes slept in the attic where the temperature on a cold winter night came close to what it was out of doors. One morning when we awoke, our breaths blowing frosty smoke, he asked what I thought of the idea of his becoming a priest. Flattered to be consulted about such a weighty matter, I gave my full and enthusiastic assent. After he went away to seminary following his third year of high school, we—my mother, father, sister and myself—visited him in North Adams, Massachusetts. He looked strange in his long cream-colored Carmelite robe, already a cleric in my eyes, making his interest in the toys I had just gotten for Christmas seem odd. A year later he would come close to dying in Korea, shot by one of the Chinese soldiers who entered the war on the side of the North Koreans, perhaps himself a former Buddhist monk.

It's noteworthy that none of us, myself included, ever felt called to the life of ordinary parish priest. The secular seminary, the one that produced clergy for parishes like our own throughout the archdiocese of Newark, was located in Ramsey, just an hour's drive from Fort Lee. Both as an altar boy and as a Boy Scout, I was taken there on outings to swim and hike and, as if coincidentally, given a tour of the seminary as well. Was there some heroic aspect to our family's vision of the priesthood that the routine of parish priest failed to satisfy? Or was our choice of the order clergy—I almost joined the Salesians, a teaching and missionary organization—just the result of our being most influenced by whatever priests we happened to be exposed to at the time we were making up our minds about whether we had vocations?

A Carmelite used to say mass at the Academy of the Holy Angels, the sprawling complex of red-brick buildings where my sister attended high school. Our parish provided altar boys for the seven o'clock mass every weekday which was attended by nuns, novices and boarders. I served that mass, as had my father thirty years earlier. The priest who celebrated it in my day, by then an old man, had been instrumental in guiding my father into a Carmelite seminary in Chicago. When my brother Donald entered the same order we were living in Englewood, a Carmelite parish. Jack, the eldest, had had his second cousin, the Maryknoll missionary, for a role model.

Even so, it was no mere coincidence of timing that drew us to the order clergy but an idealism that was also ultimately and ironically responsible for none of us—I never actually entered a seminary myself—sticking it out to ordination. The goals we set for ourselves, laid down in the first instance by a mother who viewed compromise of any kind as sin, were too high for normal human beings, even for the kind of extraordinary human beings she believed us to be. We were better than other young men, she said, not a statement of praise so much as an injunction that for this reason more was expected of us. We were called to the priesthood because, by definition, we were special. But because we had so much more to offer than ordinary young men, even ordinary Roman Catholics, she believed we had an obligation to succeed even—and this was expressed with a disappointment for her that must have been profound—when the priesthood no longer seemed a possibility. Later, in our early manhood, her imperative took the form of warning us against inferior women, women unworthy of our special destiny, though what that destiny could be once we had eliminated the priesthood from our futures was as much beyond her as it was beyond us. We knew as well as she that anything we could do after we had rejected the priesthood—or been rejected for the priesthood; it was never clear which was the case, and therein hangs a tale—would be inferior not just in degree but by several degrees of magnitude. We would supposedly marry and procreate like dumb animals, hopefully to produce out of our loins the vocations we could not find, or were too selfish to accept, in ourselves.

The question whether it was we who had failed or whether the Lord had chosen not to select us after all ("Many are called, but few are chosen"), was a critical but under-discussed aspect of our failures to become priests. Within just a few months after arriving at that old mansion in North Adams, Donald made the decision to become a brother instead of a priest, the male equivalent of becoming a nun—clergy, to be sure, but ancillary, auxiliary clergy. When he left the seminary a year later and joined the army, initially as a medic, he had joined the military equivalent of the religious brotherhood, medics having a life expectancy in combat of clay pigeons at a turkey shoot.

My father rarely talked about his own failed vocation, certainly never suggested any reason why he had left the seminary. From what I heard and overheard, the paramount reason, virtually the only reason, anyone left a seminary was sex. Sex was the main obstacle to be overcome not just for a priest or would-be priest, but for everyone. It was the main cause of sin in the world, and it was the crucial testing point for a vocation. Would God give sufficient grace to overcome our physical desires, sublimate them into productive channels? Would we find it in our hearts to cooperate with that grace when it was given? Therein lay all lingering doubts about why a vocation failed, even if the stumbling block was not sex: How much of the failure was due to insufficient grace and how much to selfishness? God always gave enough grace to overcome sin, but in the matter of doing the better as opposed to merely doing the good, our free wills were the decisive agent. Never mind that "will" as we understood it amounted to uncaused cause. We prayed for grace, for understanding, for the divine nod of approbation. If we failed to measure up, could not subdue our flesh and our selfishness, we failed not just as potential priests but in a decisive way that would affect our manhood for the rest of our lives. We dared not blame the deity for not providing enough fortitude, for He was all-loving and all-powerful and we had only to ask to receive, to knock and to have it opened to us. So, no matter how many confessors assured us that God had called us to lives as breeders, to the sacred task of procreating the Holy Roman Catholic Church, in our hearts a nagging voice would always whisper: You didn't have the right stuff.

This sense of not measuring up was the reason why my father was so quick to come forward at mass to take the place of an altar boy who had overslept. It was why Donald felt he had to march martyr-like into a shower of bullets, first as an unarmed target dispensing tourniquets and APC tablets and then as a ferocious combatant himself. It was why Jack agonized his way through night school and felt that no matter what he did with his life it would never measure up to the vocation he had either not been granted or had not been worth of. It was why my sister Rita had twelve children, nine of her own and three adopted. It was why I became a writer, because art seemed the only pursuit as worthy or as sacred as the religious life, and as such I latched onto it like a man at sea attaches himself to a piece of passing driftwood.

But, as I look up at my father's Indian-head profile in that bar on upper Broadway, it is not the face of a priest manqué I see. At that point in my life I do not yet know about his failure in the seminary. All I see is the grotesque he turns into as soon as he has taken one swallow of beer. His face becomes disfigured as dramatically as my mother's does when she cries, and the effect this change has upon me is subtle but profound. Throughout my life, any kind of drugging, even of an animal for medical purposes, becomes for me both frightening and pathetic. I fear any alteration of my consciousness as if it were a kind of death. It is incomprehensible to me why my father willingly chooses to enter such a state. If he knew what drink did to him, if only how it altered his physical appearance, would he not stay away from it? A man who spent so much time in front of the mirror carefully parting his thinning hair? A man whose dress was always impeccable, if pretentious (he favored Homburg hats, though he let my mother select his suits and ties)? Only much later would I understand he drank in order to face a situation that otherwise would have made him anxious—or perhaps not so much to face it as be able to put a face on for it, a persona that could clown and bluff its way through uncomfortable situations, never mind that the man he became with alcohol in him was much more discreditable than anything he might appear even in his most anxious and ineffectual states. But I came to this understanding only after I recognized the same feelings of inadequacy in myself. At the age of six, all I knew was that something in a beer glass could turn my father into a man both less and more than my father, something at once pathetic and monstrous.

JOHN
VI

No one's ever paid any attention to my version of anything, and I don't suppose they'll start as a result of what I write down here. Whatever I do, I'm always in the wrong. My wife never forgave me for moving her to New Jersey, even though there were nine of us living in that little house in Marble Hill, Mary and myself and the three kids and Mary's mother and two brothers, and the younger one was just five years older than our Jack. She couldn't understand why I didn't want to come home at night, why I drank and was in a bad mood most of the time. She didn't realize that if I did come home, there was less than a snowball's chance in hell of me getting anywhere near her with all those kids and grownups around, and the frustration was killing me.

Then, after we finally moved in with my own family in Fort Lee I felt so bad about losing my job on Wall Street and having to make a living as a garbage man, I drank to forget my humiliation. Mary said I should thank God I had any job at all when so many people were going hungry. She said being a garbage man was better than being unemployed, and anyways it was only temporary until the depression was over. She was right, she's always right, but she didn't understand what it was like to go from having a good job in a bank with a portfolio full of blue-chip stock and a brand new Dodge motor car, to go from that to hanging onto the back of a garbage truck and have to face all those neighbors who used to say, "There goes Johnny Seiffert. He's got a good job in the City."

My wife is a religious woman, and I respect her for that. Didn't I want to be a priest myself at one time? She believes God will provide, and so do I. But she didn't understand what it's like to have a bright future one day and be forced to face something very different the next. We lived very nicely on Fifth Avenue when I had my job in Chemical Corn Exchange and was doing a little sideline for a couple speakeasies where her brothers put in a good word for me. I drank, I admit, but everybody drank, even cops on the beat, partly just because it was against the law to drink. It was bad booze, but it was better than no booze at all. I always came home at the end of the day, and I always turned over my paycheck at the end of the week and allowed her to give me back what she thought I needed to get by. I was a happy man. I had a beautiful wife and a good job and then a baby and then another eleven months later. Comes the Crash, I'm nothing. No job, no money to pay the rent, and suddenly we're living with my wife's family in the Bronx.

"God will provide," she said when I asked how we'd manage to buy food for the kids. Her brothers were living off the few dollars they could scrape together doing odd jobs for local bootleggers.

I told her I didn't doubt He would provide, but what were we going to eat in the meantime?

But we never did go hungry. At least, the children didn't. Somehow my wife, or God, saw to that. And the drinks I had in those days never came out of any money I was able to earn working for the sanitation department or doing deliveries for my uncle's butcher shop in Manhattan where a few years later I was hired as a full-time employee and we could afford to buy the house on Cumley Terrace. I still had friends who were willing to stand me to a few beers, and some of the booze I got for doing extra work after hours or for helping someone stow a few crates of booze that had fallen off the back of a truck.

"God will provide," in fact, was Mary's answer for most of our difficulties until we moved into a home of our own and we thought we no longer had to worry about the bare necessities. Then it was, "Thanks be to God," for what we had. It wasn't until I started staying in the City two or three days at a time that she stopped thanking God. Prosperity made her miserable. She had a house of her own, a family of three after Donald came along, and plenty to eat. But it wasn't enough. She said she felt stranded in New Jersey with no one but the kids to talk to. She didn't get along with any of my relations except my mother who died a couple years after our marriage.

"Why don't you join the Ladies Sodality in the parish?" I said to her. But she told me she didn't want any part of the hicks who lived in that town. She said she wanted me to come home at night like other men and take her out to dinner once in a while. She didn't understand I had to work long hours in that butcher shop on Amsterdam Avenue and it wasn't easy traveling back to New Jersey late at night only to have to get up a few hours later to go back to work. If I drank it was because I had to in order to unwind. I won't deny that I hung out with a pretty fast crowd, but you have to remember, just a few years earlier I was rubbing elbows with big-shot politicians and Broadway stars. I was still a young man, with a young man's appetites. And after Donald came along the doctors told her she shouldn't have any more children, that it could kill her. So what was I supposed to do, force myself on a woman when it might end up killing her? We couldn't practice birth control except rhythm, and the priests were reluctant to give permission even for that.

In those days I went to confession in St. John's parish in Manhattan. Fr. Corcoran was the pastor in Fort Lee. I had served his masses when I was a kid, and my youngest, Tommy, served mass for him right up until the man died in the 1960s. He used to give sermons that made the rafters ring in the old parish church up at the end of Jones Road. I'd get the runs from hearing them. The day I made my first confession I stood outside the box listening to him thunder at the kid who went in to confess before me, the man's voice was perfectly audible through the heavy wood. The boy, his name was Alfred Keeps, I'll never forget, must have said something about committing a sin against purity, because Corcoran was hollering in his thick Irish brogue about how the boy would burn in hell if he didn't reform his ways. By the time it was my turn I had stomach cramps and only managed to work up the nerve to say anything at all because I didn't have any sins against purity to confess, just some "curse words" I'd used and even then only to myself where no one could hear. Twenty years later I was still as scared of Fr.

Corcoran as I was that day in first grade, so I started going to confession in the City whenever I had something to confess I didn't want him to hear.

I think Mary didn't believe I was going to confession at all, and to her that meant I had something to hide. She confessed regularly, every two weeks, to Corcoran. They got along like gangbusters once he found out she was Irish. She'd be in there half an hour at a time, and there was no raising of voices, either. Once she and he got tight I stayed away from the parish church altogether except for Sunday mass. Masses were too crowded for Corcoran to pick anyone out for stigmatizing, though he did make reference a couple times to men who abandoned their wives and children to cavort with the "fleshpots" of New York. That made my skin tingle, I can tell you. Everyone in that church knew me or knew some member of my family. But he never got more specific, probably because he didn't want to embarrass my wife who was sitting beside me.

I practically grew up in that church. I loved every beam of its rafters and looked on the white statues of Mary and Joseph at each of the side altars as if they were members of my family. I served mass there from the time I was seven years old right up to when I took a job in Chemical Corn Exchange when I was fifteen. I still know all the Latin responses, even though mass isn't said in Latin anymore. I taught them to my three sons so they could become altar boys themselves. Two of them went into seminary like I did, but they left just as I did too. I don't know why God didn't give any of us the grace to stick it out. We prayed for a priest, Mary and I. We never gave up hope until our youngest got married.

As I say, after I got the job in my uncle's shop I started making good money again, but that didn't seem to make Mary happy. She still felt marooned, "exiled," as she put it. You would think I'd moved her to Indiana. The seminary I went to was in the Midwest, and let me tell you Fort Lee was a far cry from that. She could hop a bus into Manhattan anytime she wanted or take the Elevated up to the Bronx to visit her mother. She took the kids into the City all the time to buy them shirts and pants for parochial school, and Hackensack was just a twenty-minute ride in the opposite direction. She hopped the 82 to go to movies there on weekdays. I used to find ticket stubs in her pocketbook when I was looking for change to get to work in the morning. And there were plenty of times she came into the City to meet me after work for a steak and take in a movie at Radio City Music Hall. It wasn't anything like the life we'd had when we lived on upper Fifth Avenue, but we never wanted for anything.

Finally, I couldn't take the bickering anymore and agreed to move back to the City. Only, I didn't realize how cramped I would feel with six of us—Tommy had come along by then—in one apartment. I grew up in a house, and even though I had four brothers and sisters plus my parents and grandfather living there, I could always go out in the back yard if I needed a breath of air, and there was plenty of woodland and a big golf course nearby. In the apartment on Kingsbridge Avenue we were pretty much all stuck with one another with no place to go unless we took a train up to Van Cortlandt Park or to Tibbett's Brook, and that wasn't much fun in winter. The older boys were teenagers by then, giving me the kind of lip you can expect from teenagers, and the money I was making in the butcher shop didn't go as far as we thought it would.

So, I started drinking heavily. I'm not making excuses. I know it was wrong, and I know I behaved badly, like the day I destroyed all of Mary's clothes, ripping them apart in a fit of anger. I was feeling the way I used to when we lived in Marble Hill with her relatives—frustrated. Nowadays just about anything goes in marriage, even for most Catholics, but back then we were supposed to toe the line, and that didn't leave much leeway for a man who was still in his prime. When we were older my wife and I slept in separate beds, twin beds, right next to each other. You don't sleep as well when you're older as when you're young. Plus you don't need each other physically the same way as when you're in your twenties and thirties. But back then on Kingsbridge Avenue, even when it was a good time of the month, I could scarcely get near her because there was always something for her to do for the kids or we were already fighting because I had come home with alcohol on my breath.

These are things Mary's never taken into consideration. Neither have my two older sons, who saw me at my worst in those days. I suppose that's the price you pay for being a father.

A couple years later we moved back to New Jersey, to the other end of Fort Lee, on Center Avenue. It was a bigger house and much more convenient to shopping. The war was over. The country was prosperous. Business was good in my uncle's shop, and I had every reason to expect he would sell the place to me at a reasonable price when he retired. But even though the shop was thriving—we were servicing a lot of wealthy people on the Upper West Side – he was tight with money. I had four children and a pretty steep mortgage to meet. But he refused to give me the kind of paycheck I needed. He said, "All in good time." He was aware of my drinking and disapproved, though he rarely said anything to me. I suppose he figured I could make up the difference between what he paid me and what I needed by simply going off the sauce. But that wasn't so easy, and besides, I felt entitled to a bit of pleasure, having to bear all those responsibilities. I got up every morning, hangover or not, and was behind the counter ready to serve customers six days a week. If I had a few beers after work, what business was that of his?

So, I got into a bad habit. I started taking money out of the till. Just a few dollars at first, but then fives and tens, whatever I thought I could pocket without my uncle's noticing. There were three other men working there. Any one of them could have been taking the money. But my uncle must have known it was me. One day I showed up for work with a head that felt like a bowling ball, and he told me he knew what I had been doing and said I was fired. I told him he was a cheap son-of-a-bitch, he could shove his job up his ass, and threw my apron down on the floor. I was a good butcher and thought I could walk into any other shop and get a job. I never liked my uncle. I knew he had hired me for his wife's sake, my mother's sister. But I was tired of working long hours and kissing his ass and getting little in return.

Only, it wasn't so easy finding another job as a butcher. They didn't say so when I went looking, but other shop owners in that part of town knew why I had been let go. They might be willing to put up with a man who drank if he came to work on time and stayed off the booze when he was on duty. But there wasn't one of them would hire someone accused of pilfering from the till.

So, I was out of work and heavily in debt, and for the first time in my life I had to take a good hard look at myself. Now I thank God my uncle fired me, because I was probably only headed for more trouble. But at the time it seemed like disaster had struck, and now it was worse than the Crash because I was a man forty-three years old, which in 1949 was a lot older than it is today.

VII

Late in his life my father told me Jesus once appeared to him in the choir loft of the old Madonna church. He didn't give details, but he assured me the Jesus he saw was "as real as you are sitting there." He also told me, when I was perhaps ten years younger, that he once spent an entire night locked in a mausoleum in Madonna Cemetery. He and some other boys had been playing in the graveyard and they had left him, deliberately or not, trapped inside one of the vaults—one of the same whited sepulchers I knew only as part of the backdrop to balmy Saturday-evening May processions. Throughout his life he suffered from claustrophobia. Some nights he came home from work literally in a sweat and trembling because the "A" train had gotten stuck in a tunnel for half an hour. Even the confinement of living in an apartment with four or five other people, though they were his own wife and children, was something he couldn't get used to. He hated being held down, restricted, blocked, even temporarily.

The significance for him of seeing Jesus face-to-face I can scarcely guess at. Surely the experience must have formed a part of his choosing to become a priest as well as a great source of confusion and remorse after he had left the seminary. Many were called, few were chosen, but how select is the group who can say they have seen Christ in the flesh? A year or so before his death, at the same age my father died, my brother Donald also saw Jesus, and from that day until his death he wore a scapular beneath his undershirt, just as he used to in his youth, its brown fabric medallion lying coincidentally very near the "scapula" bone shattered four decades earlier by a burst from the gun of a Chinese soldier in Korea.

My father also wore the scapular at various times of his life, its brown tags lying in dark contrast to his womanish-white skin. The scapular is a Carmelite sacramental, though you didn't have to be clergy to wear one. The scapular that priests and brothers wore, and I suppose Carmelite nuns as well, was a wide band of cloth with a hole provided for the head and was put on as part of their brown-and-cream-colored habit. The layman's scapular was just two small cloth squares joined by brown straps, one resting on the breast, the other between the shoulder blades. On one of the squares was a picture of Saint Dominic, on the other the Sacred Heart. Unlike the Miraculous Medal that was made of silver and never wore out and didn't even tarnish thanks to constant friction against the skin, the picture of Saint Dominic faded and the thin straps that held the two brown squares together weakened from use and body sweat, not to mention the frequent washings my mother gave them. Eventually they just fell apart. But we never threw out the pieces because that would have amounted to a sacrilege. Instead, the remains accumulated in bureau drawers along with "silver" pennies, "atomic" rings and other talismans secular and divine.

My father's revelation about the apparition he had seen was typical of his confidences: short, vague and always given long after the fact. There was, for instance, the episode of the French girl. He had been to a carnival, or perhaps it was an outing to Palisades Amusement Park, and ended up on the Ferris wheel with a young Frenchwoman. Who was she? What was she doing in a backwater like Fort Lee? Was she his girlfriend or someone he got onto the ride with more or less by accident? None of these questions occurred to me at the time of his confidence, any more than it occurred to me many years earlier to ask my mother why Abraham would meekly agree to sacrifice the boy that Sarah had gone to so much trouble to bear for him at the advanced age of ninety, or how Jesus was able to restore a blind man's sight or cure leprosy merely by his touch or a word from his mouth. My mother was a woman who believed spiders were created spontaneously out of dust that accumulated in the corners of our living room. Even at the age of five or six I recognized that as a preposterous notion, but what Jesus or Moses did was documented in the Bible as the word of God to whom nothing was hard or impossible.

My father and that French girl got stuck at the top of the Ferris wheel and the girl proposed doing something my father said was so vile he wouldn't even tell me what it was, and I didn't ask because I knew it had to do with sex. It was probably similar to what he told me an Italian grocer did with a prostitute who wandered into a store next to my great-uncle's butcher shop on Amsterdam Avenue. The woman and the Italian who owned the store did whatever they did on top of a great block of ice in the basement. I realized the ice was included by my father in his story as an indication of the depravity that lust could bring a man to—especially an Italian man. But it did not occur to me to ask how he knew about the block of ice, any more than I should wonder how Jesus knew the secret of the Woman at the Well.

These homilies were pretty much the full extent of the education my father had to offer me. For a man who once considered himself fodder for the priesthood, he seemed remarkably short on moral insight. The mandatory sex talk, which he undertook only after I had caused him public embarrassment by my appalling ignorance of the human reproductive system, consisted mostly of blushes, generalities so broad in their application that he might have been talking about something entirely different, and discrete nods of the head in the general direction of the male organ. This was par for the course for a man of his, and my own, religious upbringing. There was only one serious sin in the Catholicism we knew, and it was always "mortal"—punishable by eternal damnation.

The degree to which other sins were neglected or mentioned not at all seems stunning in retrospect. Even drunkenness, not uncommon in Fort Lee, though perhaps not as endemic as in a parish made up of a majority of Irish Catholics, was at least as great an evil as sexual licentiousness and more detrimental to good family life than "impure thoughts" or self-abuse. Yet virtually all the sermons preached in the parish church, when they were not motivational orations designed to increase the take in the collection basket, were about sex. And in case we did not get the point on Sundays, every year an itinerant Redemptorist visited the parish to preach a week-long "mission." Hellfire was the principal topic of these devotions, and the short middle-aged men who preached them were artists at their trade. Since there was only one sure way of going to hell, missions were pretty much horror shows about the evils and ultimate consequence of sex.

Those evening services included confessions, the saying of the rosary and, at their conclusion, an Exposition of the Blessed Sacrament. The latter required the presence of at least one altar boy, so that was how I came to be there. Redemptorists were my first exposure to professional showmen. They made Father Donovan's and Father Devine's weekly sermons, and even the psychotic ramblings of the parish pastor, seem like weak tea by comparison. Those preachers had a stock of jokes that were not only funny but were delivered with the perfect timing of professional comedians. The personalities of those men seemed gigantic. I marveled at their performances even as I quaked in fear of their content. But as much as I stood, or rather sat, in awe of them when they were in the pulpit, I was no less amazed by the transformation they underwent when they returned to the privacy of the sacristy. The same man who had seemed as full of inspiration and vitality as Milton Berle, Bob Hope and Adlai Stevenson combined, became a morose, even pitiable figure when he was without an audience, self-absorbed, humorless, all his energies spent.

My father's religiosity was nothing like my mother's. They coincided only on the crucial issue of sexual puritanism. But, where my father's Catholicism tolerated all the other sensual pleasures, especially food and drink, the Catholicism my mother derived from was universally austere, virtually disembodied. "I eat to live, you live to eat," she would say to her husband as he was relishing one of her Sunday afternoon pot roasts with mashed potatoes and red cabbage. She seemed to believe the human body could make do on far less than what normal human beings considered minimal nourishment—nourishment of any kind. Her emotional sustenance was as Spartan as her meals, which is not to say that either was not sufficient to maintain well-being or that her cooking was not tasty and plentiful. But, there were no frills, no snacks between meals, no excuses for not doing your duty. And, of course, "compromise" was a dirty word.

Being very much a prisoner of his flesh and hense never able to match her high moral standards, my father lived in a constant state of her disapproval. He could ignore it in some areas, such as his fondness for gooey desserts and large quantities of beer, but the moral standard she demanded of him which she herself met—though not without a heroic struggle conducted behind the scenes, I suspect—drove him to an even greater depth of self-depredation than he might otherwise have felt. Penance and fasting were the only way to get back into her good graces, and after losing his job at the butcher shop he was very much subjected to both of these. Gone were the big bags of chickens and steaks and duck eggs he used to trot home with each Friday night. We had to make do with whatever my mother could throw together on the restrictive budget she had to work with, combined with the bit of money my brother Jack brought in from after-school work in a carpentry shop.

Whatever my mother thought of New Jersey, I doubt she had no strong feelings about the prospect of losing our house on Center Avenue. She had her hands full keeping it clean and had to do it pretty much on her own. Her husband was kept busy weekends maintaining and repairing the property. She preferred apartment living, but even a city girl like herself could see that nothing short of seven or eight rooms could accommodate all six of us. Besides, Jack was now in his junior year at Fort Lee High and Donald was attending St. Cecilia's in Englewood a couple towns to the north. She would just as soon not have to pull them out and start them in new schools someplace else.

Even so, it was hard to see how she was going to manage with her husband out of work and the mortgage still due on the first of every month. There was no cushion of any kind, no savings, no stocks or bonds and no one she could turn to to tide us over until my father found work again. She pointed out this fact to him on a regular basis but in a way that sounded to him more like a complaint than a plea for help, and he reacted by assuring her he would surely find something in a week or two. When she asked where he expected this new job to materialize, he could not come up with anything more definite than that someone had told him something might be available at a place he intended to look into the next day. My mother was all for him again asking his brother-in-law for a job in the cemetery, but my father drew the line at working for his sister's brother, whom he had never liked and who treated him with a sneering tolerance that irritated more than would outright hostility.

By the end of the second month of unemployment he was still without the prospect of anything more than the rumor of a job. Until this point my mother had tried not to berate him for losing his position at the butcher shop, partly because she had warned him any number of times that if he didn't stop drinking he would in fact come to such an end and seeing her prophecy come true was punishment enough, at least for the present. But she was also afraid, not just of losing the house which, though it meant nothing more to her than a lodging for her family—one place was the same as any other when you were already living in exile—but afraid for the first time in her married life her husband might decide the situation was hopeless and abandon her with four kids and no means of support.

When her husband suggested taking in a boarder just to keep food on the table, at first she assumed he was looking for a way out of meeting his responsibilities. But then she considered that a boarder would at least save him from the ignominy of seeing his children go hungry and the desperation that might drive him to. She hated having strangers underfoot. She could barely tolerate her own relatives. But she couldn't deny the practicality of the suggestion and reluctantly agreed to let her husband put an ad in *The Palisadian*.

The ad was answered the same day it appeared. A newly discharged sailor responded in person, a good-looking fellow with a mustache like Clark Gable's. My mother was so flustered when she found him standing on our front porch, she couldn't think of anything to tell him but to come back later when her husband was home.

Matt Carson was ten years younger than my father and as different from him as any man could be. Where my father was rough and inarticulate, Matt was as soft-spoken and well-mannered as the leading man in a Western—an Alan Ladd or Gary Cooper. Matt had had two years of college before entering the service and intended to finish his education in night school under the GI Bill. He also read and—this was the most extraordinary thing about him, even apart from his Hollywood looks and well-spokenness; even I who regarded my father as a kind of subhuman viewed this trait in our boarder with suspicion—he read apparently for no other reason than pleasure: thick books about history and politics whose existence I had never suspected despite my weekly visits to the Fort Lee library, a one-room affair housed over the police station in the municipal building on Main Street. Of course, the reading of such tomes could have been purely for academic reasons, I figured, the way I was required to read a book every semester and write a report. If so, the constant presence in his hands of a volume about European history or American art was excusable, though still suspect.

He was put into the sun parlor, an extension of the living room, facing the street. He slept there on a cot behind a screen. It didn't provide much in the way of privacy, but the only alternative was to offer him one of the bedrooms on the second floor, which was out of the question because that not only would have meant moving either myself or my sister out of our rooms (my brothers were already sleeping in the attic) but such an arrangement would have meant his sleeping in close proximity to my parents. As it was he shared the breakfast table each morning with myself, my sister and my mother, my father having left the house an hour earlier to look for work and my brothers to attend school.

With two of her children present to give her emotional ballast, my mother could revert to her normal Irish hospitality, enhanced by a surge of nervous energy that kept her jumping up and down to fetch more marmalade or milk even after she had already put mountains of eggs and bacon on the table. We normally only ate that kind of breakfast on Sunday mornings, but Matt was paying for his food and my mother would have been ashamed to give him anything less. He was job-hunting too, mostly in the big insurance companies in Manhattan, and my mother assumed brain work of that order required more substantial fare than did the sort of work her husband did.

What Matt's presence did for the level of civility that obtained at that first meal of the day is hard to exaggerate. Instead of nagging me about homework not properly completed the night before, my mother was concerned only with making sure our boarder had enough toast and keeping me from disgracing her by my table manners. She ordinarily came down to breakfast in a housecoat, something with tiny flowers that was always immaculately clean but did little to show off her looks. Nor did she usually bother much with makeup until it was time for my father to return home from work. But from the first morning Matt Carson was living with us she appeared in each morning in a plain but becoming dress, her lips lightly covered with one of the bright red shades she favored.

Matt seemed to take all this for granted, not realizing she was gussying herself up for his sake. I didn't make much of it because I knew my mother never went out to the A&P or even to the corner drugstore without putting on an attractive dress and applying makeup. Her nervous energy was another matter, but neither I nor my sister seemed to think much about it. We were too impressed by Matt Carson ourselves. He took an interest in each of us children individually in a way neither of our parents did. He questioned me about what I was learning in first grade and what sort of books I liked to read. He asked my sister if she had given any thought to going to college, thereby implying she was qualified to do so. No one in my immediate family or among ancestors on either side had graduated high school, much less gone to college. My parents were straining to get my oldest brother through Fort Lee High, and it was no easy matter because he much preferred to drink beer and court girls than to crack a book. The only other passion in his life was football, at which he excelled.

But it was my mother who received the bulk of our boarder's attention, though always in a discrete and well-mannered fashion. He seemed to sense in her qualities I only came to appreciate much later in my life—a keen undeveloped mind and curiosity about a wide range of subjects from politics to history to literature. At one point he gave her a copy of *Pride and Prejudice*. Much to my surprise, she devoured it in a couple days, turning to it for a few minutes at every opportunity when she was not occupied with vacuuming or washing. I had seen her read books before, and we even had a small collection on a few shelves in our living room—*The Five Little Peppers and How They Grew*, *Pollyanna*, a full set of *Journeys Through Book Land* from which she had read me nursery rhymes, the "Adventures of Tom Thumb" and other children's literature. I was able to tell from the way she articulated old nursery rhymes that she enjoyed the play of words. And simply the fact that she considered reading to be a worthwhile activity (this was before parents began preparing children for their formal education long before they ever actually set foot in a classroom) said a great deal about her. Matt quickly picked up on these qualities in her and, within the boundaries of his position as something less than house guest but more than a stranger, he encouraged her to discuss books and ideas as they shared the same table, free of my father's dampening presence at that first meal of the day. I hated to leave for school, as fascinated by the talk as my mother seemed to be.

On school holidays, when I didn't have to rush out to make the nine o'clock bell, these conversations between our boarder and my mother continued late into the morning. Probably it was my presence that gave her the permission she needed to carry on an extended conversation with a strange man without her husband being present. She didn't have to ask me to stick around because, even though I didn't understand everything they said, I enjoyed being part of it so much that even the grasshoppers in the tall grass behind the lilacs posed no competition. I assumed the two of them continued these confabs when I was not there. More likely, after clearing off the breakfast dishes my mother began her chores around the house and Matt went off job-hunting or to the library.

I never once suspected there was anything going on between them but the mutual enjoyment of two like minds. Even after Matt moved out, leaving behind a portrait taken while he was in the service that my mother placed on the mantle in the living room where it remained for several years afterwards, I never believed he had meant anything more to her than good companionship. It was only much later when my father mentioned Matt's name in a context I did not quite understand but which made my mother turn red first with embarrassment, then with anger, that I realized what that ex-sailor must have meant to her and that her anger at whatever it was my father had suggested was proof she had never acted on her feelings, remaining always the faithful, if unfulfilled spouse.

Of course, evening meals were another matter entirely because my father was present and, while he did not seem to dislike Matt personally, he knew the man outclassed him in any number of ways and that he was too rough-cut a specimen himself for its not to show. Even if Matt had not been a college man who read books right under my father's nose, he was a war veteran, and my father, if not exactly a draft dodger, neither was he a flaming patriot. It had only been my birth that had kept him out of the draft. My mother's brothers saw active duty in either the South Pacific or Europe. My father was well aware of this and it contributed to his sense of inferiority and worship for everything Irish. But, while he could admire and even welcome his brothers-in-law into his house and give them the deference due them as defenders of the country, his feelings toward Matt Carson were more complicated. Matt made it even harder by always treating my father with the utmost deference, never venturing to speak at the dinner table unless my father addressed him first.

Matt Carson at six in the evening was not the man I saw at eight in the morning when he was encouraging my mother to tell him what she thought of Jane Austen or one of the other authors he had loaned her. My father saw those books on my mother's night table and knew where they came from. This was subversion of a very insidious kind for a man whose own reading was restricted to invoices, account books and the sports section of the *Journal American*. He did not take literature seriously as a human endeavor, but he knew some people did and he associated novels with the pornography he'd been warned against in his youth. In any case, he didn't like the influence Matt had over his wife. From his point of view, our boarder was one of those people who enjoyed a soft life. Otherwise how could he have graduated high school and even attended a couple years of college? My father had been sent out to work at the age of fifteen. His first day on the job his supervisor put a gun in his pocket and handed him a briefcase containing valuable securities and told him to get on the ferry and deliver the briefcase to someone across the river in Manhattan. From that day on he worked full-time, supporting not only himself but his mother and sisters as well. He expected his oldest son to do the same whether or not he stayed in high school, and I suspect he viewed any man who didn't behave in like manner to be something less than a man.

And now here was this pampered college boy making advances toward his wife in the insidious ways only a college boy could. Add to this the humiliation of my father's unemployment and the circumstances by which he had become unemployed in the first place, and you can imagine his state of mind. It's hardly surprising that the arguments he and my mother had—I remember her repeatedly entreating him to "keep his voice down"—while never specifically about Matt Carson, were really never about anything else for the eight or ten weeks the man lived with us.

VIII

Although it is now past noon it is still cool in the dark bar where my father no longer seems to care that my mother is waiting on the broiling sidewalk outside. He has consumed three or four beers—I've lost count—and seems ready to spend the rest of the afternoon on that barstool just as if he were back in McGwire's with his wife at home making Sunday dinner.

I tell him I have to go to the bathroom. At first he pays no attention, but when I tell him again, this time with urgency, he says the men's room is in the back. My eyes have long since grown accustomed to the low light, but the bar's far end where the only other customer is still nursing a shot and beer not only seems far away but forbidding. I ask my father to come with me. He says there is no need, that I am a big boy. So I climb down off the high barstool, my short legs numb from sitting immobile for so long. The bartender looks up from where he is drying glasses long enough to jerk his head toward a dim backlit "Men's" sign.

I have been to toilets in numerous bars. They all look and smell alike, fetid places that reek of the sickly sweet smell of the little pink or white deodorant cakes in the urinals. The urinals themselves are as tall as I am. The floor slopes toward them so steeply I have trouble keeping my balance. There is no one in there but me, but I know if someone comes in before or after I have started to urinate my sphincter will refuse to open or will abruptly close. I have the same problem at recess when there are other boys lined up behind me in the lavatory. Unless I manage to find an empty stall—and even that does not always work—I have to return to class with a full bladder and hope the teacher will excuse me during class time. When I can't have the toilet to myself in McGwire's I have the same problem. The wait till my father's willing to return home can be excruciating, but if I confess my problem he just tells me to go back to the house. I know that is not what my mother wants, so I stay with him.

But this men's room is deserted. It is also much brighter in there than in the bar, so when I come out again the place seems as dark as it did when we first arrived, dark as the Fun House in Palisades Amusement Park or the booth at the Halloween festival my elementary school puts on where, after blindfolding you, one of the older students dips your hand into bowls of wet pasta and hard-boiled eggs that are supposed to be the entrails and eyeballs of murder victims.

I am so glad to have been able to relieve myself I hardly care that my mother is roasting or that my father is intent on drinking himself into oblivion and ruining our day even before it has begun. But I immediately feel a pang of guilt for allowing myself such selfish satisfaction. To atone for it, I decline the offer of another Coca-Cola.

"Just one more," he says out of the side of his mouth, Humphrey Bogart-style, pushing his empty glass forward. I have noted before his resemblance to Bogart, especially the way they both drag hard on their cigarettes and the way the smoke drifts into their eyes. As I look up at the big face on the movie screen, I wonder why my father isn't more like Bogart in character as well. If I had a choice, I would prefer Gary Cooper for a father, someone who can outdraw everyone else and never has to take a drink except to steady his nerves. But I would settle for a Bogart-father if I could get him as he is in the movies—with a touch of pathos that encourages sympathy, not the self-absorbed, alien being my father becomes as soon as he takes one sip of alcohol.

I wait until he has finished his beer, taking him at his word that this will be the last, always taking literally what I should realize is just a statement of intention, if that. This is his third or fourth "Just one more." I believed each of them, just as I assume that dinner will be ready in my mother's "two shakes of a lamb's tail" when, ravenous after my long jaunts around the neighborhood, I smell the ham or chicken in the oven. I'm not sure how long it takes a lamb to shake its tail, but it can't be more than a minute to do so twice, and after a minute has passed I am confused when there is still no dinner on the table, that the table hasn't even been set, the potatoes are still boiling and the meat still roasting. It is like this with every new turn of phrase I hear, but even when I am already familiar with it, if someone says to me they will do something "before you know it," I expect they will be able to act before I can perceive their doing so.

But even my naive credulity has its limits. And after my father drains his glass to the last foamy drop and then lifts it in the direction of the bartender who is still reading his racing form, I know I have been lied to. A kind of holy anger fills me as I slip off the bar stool and begin walking toward the exit. I don't even look back to see if my father has noticed.

It is hard to believe it can be so bright and hot outside, so bright I can barely make out my mother standing to one side of the building's faux-Tudor facade a few yards from a big Black & Tan bus in the adjacent terminal getting ready to make the run to New Jersey and into Rockland County. As my eyes become accustomed to the glare I realize she is no longer wearing the fashionable black hat she had put on for the occasion and her tasteful gray dress has been bleached white by the fierce sun. It takes a few more moments before I realize the woman I am looking at is not in fact my mother. I turn in the opposite direction, but she is nowhere in sight. I race back into the bar and cry, "Mommy's gone!" My father turns his head halfway and curls his upper lip but says nothing.

I race outside again, but now even my faux mother has disappeared and there is no one at all on the sidewalk, not even the odd passerby. The Black & Tan bus is still idling at the front of the terminal, the driver staring listlessly at the sparse Sunday traffic on upper Broadway. The few passengers on board sit with several rows of seats separating them to avoid each other's body heat, hoping the bus will get moving soon so they can take advantage of the breeze. A couple gray Public Service buses like the ones my mother and I take to the movies in Hackensack or when we come into Manhattan to shop stand with their engines off in other parts of the station. I wonder where the drivers have gone, and this reminds me there is a coffee shop attached to the terminal.

I make my way along the whitewashed wall leading toward the back of the building, expecting the coffee shop to be closed on a Sunday afternoon. But the missing drivers in their quasi-military uniforms are inside drinking coffee. Two well-dressed black men are having a quiet conversation at the counter. Near the door, where at first she escapes my notice, my mother occupies a table by herself. She is staring out the big window at the rows of apartment buildings on the avenue beyond the terminal. A half-full cup of tea, one of those heavy pieces of thick white crockery you only find in diners, is growing tepid in front of her.

She gives no sign of recognition. I approach her cautiously, afraid to sit down lest she say I have no right to be there, myself and my father having become one thanks to my failure to retrieve him from the bar's siren call. When I fail to bring him home from McGwire's that's how she seems to regard me, as if she suspects I would prefer to sit in that damp gin mill sipping watery Coca-Cola's than eat the tasty meal she has spent most of the day preparing.

I have nothing to report now but the status quo which she knows all too well, so I say nothing. Neither does she, resuming her contemplation of the gray-brown façades of those apartment buildings a couple blocks away. It is then that I notice her eyes are moist. For a moment I think I am going to witness that terrible disfigurement that occurs when her native stoicism collapses. But each time a tear gets ready to fall she blinks it away irritably. Outside the coffee shop a bus roars to life, bringing her out of her reverie. She looks down at the half-drunk cup of tea as if it belongs to someone else. Then she turns to me.

"And what do you have to say for yourself?"

I assume she means I am to make some sort of accounting for my behavior as my father's guardian. But all I can do is stand mutely in front of her, my own eyes filling up with shame. The beginning of a smile restores her face to its usual symmetry. Standing up, she puts a dime down on the table and takes my hand in her own.

She leads me away from the fumes and heat of the bus terminal toward those apartment buildings to the south. When my father takes me to Giants baseball games in the Polo Grounds he uses a similar route after we get off the bus at that same terminal. The neighborhood is solidly black, "Negro" was the word used, and on a Sunday afternoon the men are sitting out on the stoops and sidewalks. My father gives everyone we pass a bright hello, sometimes with a quip attached, such as, "How the Jints doin' today?" The men reply with polite, circumspect nods, under no illusion about the reason for my father's sociability. To me he remarks sotto voce, "It's a good idea to act friendly in this kind of neighborhood."

But my mother has no interest in the people on the street, the few that are out on this hot afternoon. We walk south for two or three blocks, our joined hands becoming more and more sweaty. But she doesn't seem to notice. I assume she is abandoning my father to his beer and, if his friend actually does turn up, expects him to spend the rest of the day without us. I even have a notion she intends for she and I to take in a Giants game, though I can't see her sitting in the crowded stands enveloped by cigar smoke, enjoying a pastime she holds in contempt if for no other reason than it is ostensibly for its sake that her husband hangs out for hours on end in McGwire's.

She turns down one of the side streets. We head through a canyon of buildings with long narrow courtyards that stretch from the sidewalk to the entrance doorways. As we pass by those same black men my father makes a point of greeting, I smile and nod.

"What did you say?" my mother asks, thinking I've spoken to her.

"Nothing," I say, realizing that my father's idea of sociability, however self-serving, is not her own. She keeps herself to herself, and expects others to do the same.

When we reach the next avenue she stops, frowns and looks left, right and backward as if to get her bearings.

"I'm all turned around," she says, regarding a set of buildings that seem to me identical to all the others. "I thought we used to live on this corner, but I must be wrong. There used to be a church," she says, "but I don't see any church."

I look around. There isn't any steeple in sight.

"I could swear it was that building there my father was superintendent," she says, pointing. "That was where the fire was. We had to scramble to get out. It was terrible. But now I don't know if that's the place or not."

Some boys a few years older than myself leave off their stickball game and begin staring at us. I give my mother's hand a yank and say we should be moving on. But she doesn't seem to notice, her attention still occupied with the memory that has drawn her here. "I must be getting old," she says in a tired voice, and finally allows me to lead her back toward the bus terminal. But instead of heading toward the bar, we continue walking north along Amsterdam Avenue. Somewhere along the way we cut back to Broadway, then continue uptown.

This is a part of the city we are both familiar with. After Herald Square and Hackensack, upper Broadway is my mother's favorite shopping haunt. It's not just a short bus ride across the George Washington Bridge from Fort Lee, it also has a connection to a bus that takes us up to Marble Hill, where my grandmother lives. We visit her every couple months and make special trips for her birthday or St. Patrick's Day, stopping in the florist just below the 225th Street elevated station to pick up a potted flower or, when nothing special is required, a cake from one of the bakeries along Broadway.

But those excursions are always undertaken on weekdays when the dress shops whose windows my mother loves to study are open for business and the fruit stands instead of being shut up tight as they are today are overflowing with ripe oranges, pears, apples and long strings of bananas. Those days I have to stay close to my mother and be sure not to let go her hand lest I become lost or crushed in the crowds of big-hipped women squeezing tomatoes with that peculiar city energy so lacking in Fort Lee.

But there are scarcely more than half a dozen people on any given block this afternoon, and they are strolling along as if with no purpose in mind. The contents of the shop windows are clearly visible because this is an age before burglary gates are required, but my mother's interest is not peaked the way it is during our weekday excursions when the street life is as much a lure as any of the items in the shop windows.

I ask if we're going to visit grandma, but she doesn't reply. Even so, I feel content just being with her, far more so than I ever feel with my father who is in a sense more my charge than I am his. It is no small responsibility for a six-year-old to be held accountable for a man thirty-five years his senior. When I recall that he is still sitting in that dark bar next to the bus terminal, he seems far remote from the hot concrete beneath my feet or the sweaty pressure of my mother's hand on my own. But I still feel a thrill in my gut, a frisson of wickedness or delight, the same feeling I get when my tricycle goes over a sudden rise in the sidewalk or when I recall something shameful I've done that I dare not tell my mother but carry around with me week after week like a sore that won't heal but which I can't refrain from scratching and keep fresh. I have a sense that this day will end badly, as if I were watching one of those movies that first shows a speeding car careening across the screen left to right, then cuts to another car moving at the same breakneck speed in the opposite direction. But I can't quite make out what the two objects are that are headed for destruction that afternoon except that they're of a piece with the evil spirit that inhabits those fluted beer glasses my father insists on having filled and refilled and the deep sense of obstinacy and resentment my mother harbors in her heart like someone who has been condemned to a long prison term for a crime she did not commit.

She takes me to a diner, a hole-in-the-wall sandwiched in between a newsstand and a secondhand clothing store. I order a hamburger. She frowns because she knows what I am about to eat is not as healthy as the lean meats she prepares for me. She asks if I wouldn't like a nice grilled cheese instead, but I can already taste the greasy meat. It must be past one p.m. by now, and I'm starving. She orders nothing herself, content with the Spartan nourishment of that half cup of tea she drank at the bus terminal. The counterman, a stout bald middle-aged fellow in a white T-shirt smiles at her boldly, exposing a bright gold tooth.

I ask if I might have a piece of lemon meringue pie for dessert. She allows this without comment, only insisting that I finish the tall glass of milk that came with the hamburger. This treat—a burger and pie—make up for the anxieties I suffered in that dark bar on her behalf. Earlier that day I attended the children's mass in the old church at the other end of town. Sometimes after the long walk there following a fast which began at six the previous evening, our weekday dinner hour, I become lightheaded during the ceremony and one of the nuns takes me outside and has me put my head between my knees. It isn't until I get back home and have a bowl of Cheerios that I feel like myself again. Ordinarily, my mother has the same problem going without food, but today either because of the heat or the aggravation she's enduring, she seems to have no appetite.

She pays the tab and leaves a shiny new dime next to my plate. The counterman thanks her with another flash of gold tooth. Outside it seems even hotter than before, and the combination of heat and heavy food stupefies me. I follow her along the sidewalk, stopping where she stops to admire something in a shop window, then moving on again as if I am on a train or a ship whose motion is entirely out of my control. It is only after we have crossed Broadway and walked a few blocks south that I realize we're heading back toward that bar on 168th Street. And, suddenly, it is not the leisurely walk past the beautifully designed display windows or the hot pressure of my mother's hand on my own that seems real but, again, the damp rancid smell of that dark gin mill.

JACK
IX

I'm Jack, the oldest.

There's three years between me and Donald, slightly less than a year between me and Rita, a full twelve between me and Tommy. It's almost as if we older children are a different generation from him. I grew up in the '30s and early 1940s. Tommy scarcely remembers the second world war, if he remembers it at all. If I had been born a few years earlier I would have fought on a beach in Normandy or sweltered in a foxhole in the South Pacific. As it is, I joined the Navy in 1947 a couple years shy of my graduation from Fort Lee High School where I was named all-county tackle that year.

The man I remember as my father is not the same one Tommy remembers. The John Seiffert I grew up under was a hard-drinking, cruel man who didn't think twice before taking his belt or something stronger to me. Mary wasn't much better, the two of them both had terrible tempers and they took out their frustrations as much on the kids as they did on each other. In those days the old man was gone for days, sometimes weeks at a time, and Mary would go crazy with anxiety and anger. If you crossed her over the least thing she would reach for whatever was handy, a broomstick, a spatula, even a baseball bat. I had welts on me that made me look like something out of a Nazi prison camp. Neither of them lit into Rita or Donald like that. I was a wild kid, I suppose, but I vowed I'd never beat a child of my own that way, and I never have.

I was born in Manhattan. All my early memories are of the City, mostly of my grandmother's house in Marble Hill where we lived for a couple years, but also of the apartment on Kingsbridge Avenue where we moved after my parents sold the house on Cumley Terrace. I started school in St. John's on Broadway, then transferred to Madonna in Fort

Lee. It wasn't easy making the switch from the Bronx to what was then just a small town that could have have been located in Indiana instead of just across the Hudson from New York City. The day we moved, Donald and I stood watching the men unload our furniture from the back of the van. We noticed a couple neighborhood kids watching. They weren't doing anything or saying anything, just watching. But we didn't like the looks of them, and that was a good enough reason to start a fight. That was our inauguration into small town life, and it pretty much continued that way all through our childhood and adolescence.

I've tried over the years—I'm now a man of 70—to come to terms with my anger toward the old man. But it not only persists, it seems to grow deeper the older I get. I should be mellowing out, finding reasons to forgive, especially since my own life has not exactly been spotless. But just the opposite seems to be happening. I hate him. I always hated him. Not just for the way he treated me when I was young, and the beatings were only part of it, but because of the sort of man he was—selfish, venal, ignorant. When I was fifteen, just back from a year in seminary and having a hard enough time paying attention to my studies, he told me it was time I got a job and became self-supporting. He said he had "carried" me for the first decade and a half of my life. Now it was time for me to begin pulling my own weight. I didn't question the rightness or wrongness of what he said, I just went out and found a job as a carpenter's apprentice and worked three or four hours after school every afternoon and all day Saturday. I turned over my entire paycheck to my mother.

From that day on I decided to live my life apart from him, and if that meant also living it apart from the rest of the family, so be it. I was popular in school and had plenty of girlfriends. Between them and my athletic success I led a pretty active social life, you could say. I drank a lot for a kid of sixteen. Sometimes when I came home half in the bag I found the old man waiting up for me. When he saw the condition I was in he would slap me around for a while. But that stopped after I started to fill out and became capable of knocking him on his ass if I chose to. I'll never forget the first time I pushed him back when he came at me with his open hand. He was so startled, I might have been a stranger he had mistaken for his flesh and blood. After that whenever he took a step toward me, I took a step toward him, and it was always he who backed off. From that point on I lost whatever respect I still had for him. It wasn't long after that I decided to join the Navy, though it was just a few weeks till I would have had my high school diploma.

It was different for Donald because he was his mother's favorite. The old man knew it and left him alone. Donald also learned early on, much earlier than me, that the only way to get away from the angry feelings we had was to stay away from the old man. Donald learned to keep to himself. Later, after his hitch in the military, it was a different matter and there was a major blowup. But that was still several years in the future, and it really had more to do with Donald and his mother than it did with him and his father.

Rita was a girl and a special case, you could say. She might have been more traumatized than any of us by the goings-on in that family, but of course the old man never struck her. In fact, he treated her as if she were a fragile object that might break if he so much as looked cross-eyed at her. When she was a baby he carried her around on a pillow because he was afraid her little bones might shatter. She was the only one of us three to graduate high school in four years and she did so from the Academy of the Holy Angels. Holy Angels wasn't your ordinary Catholic high school. It was a fancy girls academy for the well-to-do. Rita was the smartest one in the family and could have gone on to college. But most girls in those days ended their educations with high school unless they chose to become nuns, and for a while Rita did entertain a notion in that direction. I don't know exactly why she didn't go into the convent. It wasn't just because she was in love with Tim McCullough. Her best friend Susan Cafferty had a boyfriend, but Susan went into the convent and is still there as far as I know, if she's alive. In those days, being sexually normal was no impediment to having a vocation. If anything, it meant you had something to give up that made your calling even more valuable in the eyes of God.

I once thought I had a vocation myself, but now I wonder if going away to that minor seminary in Akron wasn't just my way of my getting out of that house. At the time, though, I believed I wanted to be a priest. I had not only been an altar boy, I was master of ceremonies at all the major high masses conducted in the old Madonna Church. It seemed a short and logical step to move on from being chief altar boy to becoming the celebrant who changed bread and wine into the body and blood of Christ.

Like most other young men who thought they had a vocation to the priesthood, I had no illusions about my sexuality, which by the age of fourteen was pretty well developed. But doing without sexual love, I thought, would be just one more offering to lay on the altar along with my vows of obedience and poverty. It's hard for young people today to imagine how attractive that kind of sacrifice once seemed to people like me and for the generations that came before mine. It's all different now, with the high rate of homosexuality in the clergy and the revelations about priests molesting children and having girlfriends.

A friend of mine who knows something about these things told me fully half the priests in his diocese consort with women on a regular basis. However well-concealed such behavior may have been forty or fifty years ago, no one can convince me it went on to any great extent. Which is not to say there weren't priests for whom the vow of celibacy was difficult. Even as a kid I saw the strain in some of them, though at the time I didn't recognize it for what it was. On a conscious level I thought celibacy was a kind of gift and they actually were free of longings that plagued young men like myself. Psychologists have another name for that kind of abstinence, but I'm not sure it matters whether you call it a "gift," "sublimation" or something else. Back then that kind of self-denial represented a high degree of idealism. If you offer something noble and difficult to young people, some will always respond. By today's standards that world was parochial, puritanical, even unhealthy. But you can't judge one generation by the standards of the next.

I joined the Navy. I was just a few weeks shy of graduation—May, 1947. I didn't have the highest grades in the world, just a talent for tackling other young men on the football field. Otherwise college meant nothing to me, just a place where rich people sent their kids to horse around for a few years before joining the family business.... That's a bit of an exaggeration. I actually had a notion of going to law school—nothing more than a notion, though. I didn't dare try to see it realized. It was as if I knew such an ambition was well beyond someone like myself, an aspiration I had no right to entertain. The truth is, I lacked the confidence to follow through on such an idea.

Over the years I've spent a lot of time thinking about that decision to quit school and join the service. It wasn't until much later when I was attending St. Peter's College nights that I first came across Arthur Miller's *Death of a Salesman*. I had missed the movie with Frederick March because it came out, I think, just after I went into the service. The parallel between what happened to Biff Loman and my own experience is uncanny. I've taught that play any number of times during my years as a high school teacher. Tears still come to my eyes when I read the scene where Willie and his son confront each other just before the boy leaves home for good. It's the combination of love and resentment and disappointment that gets to me. There was nothing in my experience that corresponds to Biff's discovering his father had a woman on the side, shattering the illusion he had constructed around the man. But the combination of details—Biff's being the first-born son with a brother a few years younger, his great success as a high school football star and the overpowering presence of his father in his life—it seemed as if the play had been written about me and my old man.

I suppose millions of Americans must be able to relate to that play like I did. After almost forty years of teaching I can verify many do—white kids, black kids, Jewish kids, it doesn't matter. But as I sat on the bus during one of the long rides to my college in Jersey City, reading the first scenes of that play I became so agitated I thought I might have to get off. It seemed as if the playwright had somehow gained access to the most intimate details of my life. I didn't even know yet the play had been produced, never mind been a big hit on Broadway and a movie besides. To me, it was as if I had discovered that a perfect stranger had written a story specifically about me and my father.

I've spent a lot of time thinking about *Death of a Salesman*. But it wasn't until recently that it struck me it wasn't necessary for that scene to occur between Willie and his son where the boy discovers his father in adultery. It may be necessary dramatically but not in real life, and I'm living proof. The source of my resentment toward the old man was a long accumulation of beatings and humiliations and seeing him in states that can only cause a child to lose respect for a parent. By comparison, Willie Loman was a model parent.

The Navy was a lot like high school except I didn't have to come home each night, which was all to the good, and of course I wasn't a star anymore. But nobody else was either. In boot camp we were all new recruits, and I did as well as anyone—swimming under burning oil, climbing ropes, that sort of thing. I had no particular ambition to rise in the ranks and never made it past seaman first-class. But I enjoyed much the same sense of camaraderie I did in Fort Lee High.

There were no girls, of course, except for shore leave. But, leave was worth waiting for, because we were assigned to the Mediterranean. We put in at Nice and Naples and Athens and any number of other ports where a young man had no trouble finding a good time. I served on a carrier and was kept as busy as in any job I would subsequently hold in civilian life. I enjoyed being at sea and got along with my shipmates as well as most of the officers. I only saw my family once a year. My mother and sister made a great deal of me in my uniform, and my girlfriend Charlotte cried each time she saw me off at Pennsylvania Station. And in between those visits I had a pretty good time for myself.

After my discharge it was a different story.

X

My fondest early memory of him is of a young man appearing late at night in my bedroom to present me with a new set of silver cap pistols in white leather holsters. It was probably my birthday, although the pistols may have been a get-well present. I was frequently ill.

He couldn't have been more than sixteen, which makes me four at the time, but he was already earning money. Until the day she died my mother still had the desk he made for her. In his twenties he refinished it and gave it several new coats of shellac, buffing each new application with steel wool in the garage behind the house where we rented a second-floor apartment. That was the summer before he went away to graduate school after completing his college degree nights.

My other early memories of him are just as dramatic: rescuing me from the bathroom on Cumley Terrace when I was two or three and had locked myself in and was unable to figure out how to release the lock. He was painting the back side of the house that day and had a ladder handy. He put it beneath the bathroom window and, talking through it, first calmed me down, then explained how to go about unlocking the door.

Later, in the house on Center Avenue where he presented me with those beautiful pistols, I liked to fill the bath tub with water, add washing detergent, shampoo, baking soda or whatever I could lay my hands on, before stepping into the mix. I had experienced no ill effects until the afternoon I must have added something caustic because as soon as I sat down in the mix I jumped up, my private parts on fire. I stood howling on the bathroom floor until Jack miraculously appeared and, taking in what had happened on his own, laid me down on the bathmat and applied moist washcloths to the affected area, affording instant relief.

He was—still is—that sort: the person you want around when there's a crisis. In his sixties, when he made a trip to Germany after years of putting it off despite making so much of his German ancestry as if to compensate for his father's bad-mouthing it, he and his wife were sitting in a restaurant when someone at a nearby table began choking. Jack got up from his plate of *brauten* and applied the Heimlich maneuver to the choking man as if he did that sort of thing every day.

Later, in my teenage years, he came to my rescue in a very different way when it seemed my fate would also be the seminary. After getting his high school equivalency diploma, he enrolled as a night student in St. Peter's, a one-and-a-half-hour bus trip from Fort Lee. The long commute gave him a chance to study, as did his hours sitting on a cab line at the George Washington Bridge plaza where he spent much of his out-of-class time working for a local car service. He quickly bought into the Jesuit idea of education and promoted it to my parents while I was still in elementary school. By the time I was in eighth grade there was no question about whether I would attend a Jesuit high school, only whether it would be St. Peter's Prep or one of the Jesuit schools in New York. As it turned out, it was the prospect of the long bus trip he had endured for so many years that led to my opting for a school in the Bronx.

But getting me into a Jesuit high school would not have been enough to keep me out of seminary. Jesuits didn't openly proselytize for recruits—it was against their rules to do so. But the idea, not to say the ideal, was always in the air and was discussed discreetly during week-long "retreats" when the Jesuits had us all to themselves away from the distraction of families and girlfriends and could impress upon us not only the deadly dangers of masturbation and sex generally but portray the shining alternative of a life spent in the service of the Savior of mankind. Ironically, it was a Jesuit who was ultimately to rescue me from the seminary by writing a note at the end of one of my first attempts at short story writing indicating I should consider becoming a professional writer. That was all the escape hatch I needed—a vocation every bit as useful and noble as that of consecrating bread and wine or forgiving someone's sins in a dark confessional. I latched onto it.

But it was really Jack who gave me the nerve to say no to the priesthood. He and I had long conversations, not just about my future as a writer but about all sorts of topics I was interested in but never dreamed I could share with anyone else. We talked philosophy, religion, politics – those were the days of the McCarthy hearings. Those conversations with my brother were my first taste of the intellectual life, and much of Jack's pitch for Jesuit education was based on the prospect of a career spent awash in ideas and the pursuit of truth. Except for my junior year in high school, when I was taught by that young man who suggested I pursue a career as a writer, the Jesuits did not live up to Jack's billing. But his own companionship never flagged. From the earliest days of his discharge from the Navy until he left home to attend graduate school in the University of Maryland, I played Boswell to his Johnson and loved him with a passion only a boy of that age can feel for an intelligent and handsome older brother.

The same year of his release from the service he became engaged to my sister's best friend, a graduate of the Academy of the Holy Angels whose family owned a house in exclusive Englewood Cliffs. One afternoon Jack decided to walk there from Fort Lee and invited me to tag along. We took Jones Road, then little more than a country lane leading past the old Madonna Church and ending a few miles north among the estates of millionaires. As we walked I discovered he was actually interested—or at least seemed not unwilling to listen—to what I had to say. And I talked non-stop, unburdening myself of all the thoughts and opinions I didn't even know I had stored up and had had no one to share them with.

That day was the first time I had seen him with a woman since his high school sweetheart used to see him off from the old Pennsylvania Station in Manhattan after one of his shore leaves. My father and mother drove him there in our old Dodge. Jack and Charlotte had the back seat to themselves, but I could see in the rearview mirror by taking glances over my shoulder, for which I was reprimanded by my mother with a smile that made me wonder how that sort of thing could be forbidden so vigorously by our religion and yet smiled on by a woman like my mother. They necked all the way to Penn Station, and then again after my parents had said their own goodbyes and stood at a discrete distance as the train steamed and hissed on the platform. All the way back to Fort Lee Charlotte wept buckets of tears, something I had seen no woman do for any man outside the dark confines of those Hackensack movie theaters.

The only other times I saw Charlotte was at Sunday dinners when she sat very upright and ill-at-ease. She was a very pretty girl, with big brown eyes, dark hair and the whitest complexion I had ever seen. Throughout the meal Jack was extremely attentive to her, spooning food onto her plate as if he were caressing her and whispering in her ear. Later, I would try to behave toward my own girlfriends with the same devotion to such simple matters and, to this day, heaping mashed potatoes onto a woman's plate while murmuring sweet nothings to her seems about the most romantic thing a man can do.

By the time we took that hike to Englewood Cliffs, Charlotte had faded into the past—at least into my past, though their song, Vaughn Munro's "Dance, Ballerina, Dance" could agitate my brother well into his middle age. I had received only a few letters from him during his years with the Sixth Fleet, but in each there was a promise to send me something from one of his exotic ports of call—a fez from Morocco, a guitar from Spain (I turned down it, afraid I would not do it justice) a book of Greek stamps some of which turned out to be valuable.

We were no sooner inside his fiancée's house, a ranch-style affair set well back from the road by a circular driveway and sequestered by a jungle of trees and shrubbery, than Mariena, a woman hardly taller than myself, planted herself on his lap. Till then I had only known her as my sister's best friend. I knew she was rich—her father owned a popular line of canned olives. Every year his daughter received a new Oldsmobile for her birthday which, as any rich girl should, she drove well above the speed limit on our local streets. She had wiry dark hair and a complexion as dark as the Sicilians' in the poorer section of Fort Lee, and was not especially pretty. That day she was sporting the engagement ring my brother had bought her, a speck of diamond that was nevertheless more than he could afford, admiring it as proudly as if it were something a queen might covet.

She put a record on the phonograph, a Chopin waltz. When she was still just my sister's friend, she once asked what I wanted for my birthday. I told her a recording of Perry Como's "Till the End of Time" whose melody I could not get out of my head. She gave me instead a seventy-eight rpm disk of the Chopin polonaise whose theme was stolen for that song. Such was my introduction to classical music, and although my brother always had a talent for the piano—he taught himself to play by ear—it was Mariena who put him on to classical music. When my parents bought an RCA phonograph capable of playing thirty-three rpm's as well as the old seventy-eights, he began putting together a collection of recordings. Given my love for music—I felt on the verge of levitation when Sister Marie Therese launched into the War March of the Priests after Sunday children's mass—you could say Mariena was as responsible for my musical education as she was for my brother's.

But even as I watched with amazement the familiarity with which the woman had parked herself on my brother's lap, I could see something was wrong. He was not responding with the debonair confidence he had shown when he was spooning vegetables onto Charlotte's plate. Nor did I sense any great ardor on his part, though Mariena seemed as happy as any young woman with the prospect of matrimony in her immediate future.

A couple weeks later he broke off the engagement. Ostensibly it was because Mariena had published an announcement in the local newspaper without his consent. But there was something forced about his indignation, suggesting another, less superficial reason for the rupture. There were long talks with my mother about what action could be taken if Mariena did not return the engagement ring. I don't recall my sister's attitude, though she should have been conflicted between loyalty to her friend and to her brother. But in a crunch there would have been no contest: She was as much in love with Jack as Mariena or Charlotte had ever been. She once told me that if she weren't his sister she would gladly have him for a husband.

That was the last time I saw Mariena. For decades afterward she tried to maintain contact with our family, at least with my mother to whom she always sent Christmas greetings and a birthday present even after she had married and was raising a family of her own. My mother kept her at arm's length, suspecting her intention was to get my brother back, something no good Catholic mother could be party to. But she tolerated the occasional telephone call which, however uneasy they made her, felt touched no doubt by the woman's affection for here.

When I was older and better understood the social implications of marriage, I thought about how Jack's life would have been different if he had married Mariena. He certainly would have come into what for our family was great wealth. His exposure to classical music and to culture in general would have been enhanced. Whatever the cause for his breaking off the engagement—I came to suspect it was a combination of cold feet and lack of love for the woman—it would be many years before he made a serious attachment to any other woman.

XI

When we get back to the bar my father is standing on the sidewalk outside swaying like a newly risen Lazarus. Beside him stands a smallish man in a gray suit and Fedora.

My father says my mother and I have been holding up the proceedings by our absence. His friend, whom my father introduces as "Gus" only after the man prompts him, regards my father with nervous amusement. He looks to be par for my father's suddenly-acquired and quickly-disposed-of acquaintances. He is regarding my father as he might a difficult, possibly volatile older brother. Even my father's semi-inebriate state does not so much put the man off as confuse him, as if my father were a disappointing stand-in for the man with whom he has arranged to share the afternoon.

My father hails one of the numerous Yellow Cabs careening up Broadway, an old Checker whose backseat can accommodate a small army. He, not Gus, gives directions to the driver, a thin elderly black man who reacts with so many "Yes, boss"es and servile grins that it's obvious he's wary, if not downright fearful, of his two passengers. Gus has apparently put himself into my father's hands, though it's to Gus's house we are traveling and my father is a good deal less sober than his host. Just as I've seen my father bully his brothers by the mere force of his personality, however alcoholically powered, that same force now seems to be cowing Gus. It's only my mother who is strong enough to stand up to him when he is in this mood (in a sober state there is no contest, and he knows it). She will go toe to toe with her husband, eyeball to eyeball, never retreating an inch or conceding a single point. He makes feeble, pathetic attempts at self-justification, complains of her lack of consideration, her excessive self-righteousness, even makes reference to a mysterious lack of feeling for him in terms so heavily veiled that I don't understand what he meant until I am an adult myself. For a while, until she has begun to wear him down behind the impenetrable shield of her probity, he seems to hold his own. But it

isn't long before the thin armor of his self-pity is breached and he is
backing off, literally and rhetorically, having to defend himself now not
against her original accusations of irresponsibility and general moral
failure but against lesser barbs that seem to pierce the flimsy courage of
his drunkenness more effectively. "You always manage to bring that up,
don't you?" he whines. "You never let an opportunity pass. You'll never
let that one die, will you."

Of course, I have no idea what "that one" is, though I'm full of
curiosity despite the terror with which I observe these encounters, a
reaction as inevitable as the stomach-aches when I eat too fast or try
to down more cherries or grapes than are good for me. "That one" is a
grievance with which she can be sure to wound, halt him in his tracks
no matter what the immediate subject of their argument. It comes up
every time they have a disagreement, arises even when there is none,
when, for instance, we are guests at someone's house or are entertaining
company at home. Suddenly the two of them are going at each other,
embarrassing everyone present, until the dinner or whatever the affair
happens to be is ruined.

Somewhere in upper Manhattan my father's friend attempts to give
directions to the taxi driver, but my father cuts him off with his own
orders, making the driver grin nervously, the dark eyes I see in the
rearview mirror darting rapidly from one to the other white man in the
back seat.

"You want me to take the *Washington* Bridge?" the man says.

Both men object vigorously to this idea, thinking the man intends
to drive us back to New Jersey rather than across the Harlem River
and into the borough of Queens. Perhaps it is this prospect, on top of
everything else he is about to endure, that gives my father's friend the
power to find his voice.

"No, no," the driver assures him, putting as much force into his
reply as he dares, "I mean the *new* Washington Bridge."

By now we are safely crossing the river, so both my father and his friend both sit back and laugh.

"'The *new* Washington Bridge,'" my father echoes in the mocking tone he uses to imitate black speech, with none of the cautious deference he exhibits when we're taking that shortcut to the Polo Grounds. "That's okay, then," he says. "You just keep driving, boss."

I'm used to riding in the backseat when my father takes us for a Sunday afternoon excursion into Rockland County or the northwestern reaches of New Jersey. But even when he is three sheets to the wind, as he usually is after a few stops to "use the bathroom" at bars along the way, it is he and not someone else who is doing the driving. And I always have the backseat to myself. Today both my parents are not only accompanying me in the rear of the taxi, but I sit facing them and Gus on the low jump seat as if it were I who was the adult keeping an eye on three troublesome children. Of course, only one of them is troublesome. The other two endure his antics like classmates embarrassed by the misbehavior of a fellow student but unable to do anything about it.

The terrain of the Bronx is not totally unfamiliar. I've been taken here to visit the zoo or to see one of my uncles' or aunts' families. It's a landscape of concrete canyons, nothing like the scenes I'm used to from our Sunday drives in the country. Those rural excursions rarely end up anywhere, unless it's to stop at a subdivision under construction where my parents pretend to be prospective buyers looking over what's on offer. My father's typical route is a big loop up Route 17 to Suffern or just south of there—for some reason, the sign indicating the city limits seem to be a warning that he's gone far enough—and back again. Only rarely, with no previous planning and always on the spur of the moment, do we venture further, down to the Jersey Shore for an overnight in some seedy rooming house or, once, up to Lake George, an all-day trip on US 9W. My mother doesn't object, though not only does she not have a bathing suit at the start of these impromptu adventures, she doesn't even have a change of underwear. We buy both after we get there.

We leave the high-rises of the Bronx behind and enter a genteel section of Queens. The architecture, though suburban, looks totally unfamiliar, row- and semi-detached houses, a species of dwellings unknown in our part of Bergen County. We soon leave these behind as well and enter an area that looks more like what I'm used to: wood-frame houses with wrap-around porches and broad expanses of lawn in front and back. Our taxi pulls into the driveway of one of these and my mother and father—who has fallen asleep and is roused only with difficulty—follow our host up a narrow flagstone walk bordered by battalions of bright red flowers.

The house's outermost door is glass and controlled by a pneumatic device so powerful it knocks me off my feet after my father passes through. Inside is a second, screen door and only then the heavy wooden entrance door, which has been left open. The interior of the house is cool and dark and smells like the damp tool shed beneath our front porch where my father stores his bags of sand and cement. The furniture is neither the modernistic style my mother favors—always bought on credit—nor the plastic-covered baroque of my friends' houses, rooms the children are never allowed to play in, much less bring friends into.

We're offered cold drinks by Gus's wife Brenda, a slim talkative woman with bright yellow hair whose gregariousness makes up for her husband's shyness. My father chooses beer. My mother looks ill-at-ease and angry as she usually does under these circumstances. Her husband rarely takes her anywhere, and when he does it's usually a wedding or wake where she already knows most of the people. She rarely finds herself in a totally strange living room. I note her discomfort without recognizing it is akin to the same feeling I get when I find myself in similar circumstances. Her discomfort makes me feel oddly at ease, as if she is suffering for both of us.

She accepts a lemonade from Gus's wife, toward whom my father has warmed up to immediately. He begins making silly jokes to which she responds to with a loud laugh, causing my mother's mouth to purse in irritation. She and Brenda's husband sit at opposite ends of the room, passive spectators to the light flirting their spouses are engaged in.

"Johnny," Brenda says, "you're a card is what you are."

Meanwhile, the grill is working in the backyard in anticipation of our arrival, with stacks of raw hamburgers and franks piled to either side. We're invited to adjourn there, myself, my mother and Gus with our lemonades, my father with his beer and the hostess with something tall and frosty. The sun is still fiercely hot, but there's a tall apple tree under which it is pleasant. I have never been so near a real apple tree and marvel at the proliferation of fruit both on the branches and the ground. I ask if I may take home some of the fallen apples, to which I get an immediate reproach from my mother but a hearty, "Go ahead, Tommy," from Brenda. "Take all you want!"

How my father can drink so much beer and eat besides is beyond me. Whenever he has allowed me a couple sips of his beer I always became bloated and lose my appetite. But he wolfs down two hamburgers and a hotdog, not to mention a hefty mound of homemade potato salad. The more he eats, the more his friend's wife urges on him. My mother takes one bite of the potato salad and puts it back down. All she ends up eating is single hamburger patty without the bun.

Gus seems to know the kind of woman he's married to and accepts his role as quiet partner. He pulls his lawn chair near to my mother's and begins to engage her tentatively in conversation. At first she seems reluctant to have anything to do with anyone associated with this dreadful afternoon, but she's too well-mannered not to respond to the man's respectful comments.

When I get tired of collecting fallen apples, I discover a croquet set in another part of the yard which Gus's wife encourages me to play with. I have eaten both a hamburger—my second of the day—and a frankfurter and am feeling sluggish. But my father goes on eating and drinking as if there is no bottom to him, still carrying on with Brenda as if they were old chums, making her break out in occasional gales of laughter that cause my mother's brow to become more pinched, though she refuses to look in their direction.

The afternoon is interminable, even longer than the never-ending Sundays I ordinarily spend roaming vacant lots in our neighborhood, looking for garter snakes and grasshoppers, only returning home mid-afternoon for the beef roast or leg of lamb. I spend the rest of those Sundays at the town's athletic field, where there is always a doubleheader that won't end until sundown or the men in their soiled uniforms are too tired or drunk to continue. But the sun is still bright and hot when my mother decides it's time to leave. I have long since stopped paying attention to the adults, having found other diversions besides the croquet set: a garage full of tools and gadgets whose uses I can only guess at; a set of wooden darts whose feathers are so delicate they could only have come from real birds; a red-anthill; a scooter so rusty it makes a crunching sound when I stand on it and refuses to move no matter how hard I push.

It's only when my father gets up to walk outside to the cab Gus has called that I realize how drunk he is. Though he keeps trying to push his host away, Gus has to steer him down the driveway. My mother follows, looking as if my father were someone she is not responsible for beyond transporting him back to his home in New Jersey. Brenda declares a good time was had by all and we should do it again sometime. My mother manages a cynical smile. When her hostess says, "Come again, Mary," she merely pulls the back door of the cab closed with a slam.

XII

Running through Fort Lee north to south, leaving a deep crevice like a scar left by a giant knife, was an old trolley cut, in my day a wide gully overgrown with all the local fauna including blueberry bushes and wild cherry. No one had attempted to fill it in, not even the developers who were turning what we used to call "the Gardens"—the town dump—into an upscale residential neighborhood after the second world war. For some reason they left the trolley cut as it was, a ditch less than half the width of a municipal thoroughly reclaimed by nature. Hummingbirds made their homes there along with species of bird rare to our part of the world – orioles and cardinals. Stray cats and dogs felt secure from human predators in its deep undergrowth, though in other parts of town I occasionally came upon their bloated or frozen carcasses. If that gully had been deemed haunted or filled with poisonous vegetation, it could not have been more thoroughly neglected.

The trolley cut was just one of the parts of Fort Lee then still in a more or less wild state. Opposite the garden apartments we moved into a couple years after my parents sold our house on Center Avenue, there was a square block of undeveloped land I and my friends used as a baseball field. Further in, the terrain became wooded, even densely so. In its depths was a marshy pond where garden snakes by the dozens sunned themselves on tall reeds, paying no mind to our attempts to shoot them with our bows and arrows.

Further west, across Anderson Avenue, was the Great North Woods, a few square miles of undeveloped real estate, virgin woodland with a small lake full of tadpoles, paramecia and other macro- and microscopic life forms that were my obsession for a while. The Boy Scouts used the Woods as a camping site. In the early 1950s a fire broke out there that burned for weeks. Even after it was put out above-ground it continued to smolder under the soil which remained as hot as if it were the roof of purgatory. For several weeks you could be abruptly confronted by a tree suddenly bursting into flame, as spectacular and miraculous an event as anything in the Old Testament.

It was along that gully bifurcating town like a seismic fault that my father once rode the trolley south to Cliffside Park, back before the internal combustion engine became the preferred means of mass transportation. He rode it south to Cliffside Park and then down to the Hudson River where he boarded a ferry to Manhattan. Other trolley lines ran east and west and in my time were covered over by macadam. But in my father's youth you could not only take a trolley to any number of locales north and south of Fort Lee, but it was said that by means of free transfers you could journey all the way to Chicago—for just a nickel.

The ferry docked at Manhattan's 125th Street, the neighborhood from which the Seifferts had migrated to New Jersey. Perched on the cliffs just across the river, Palisades Amusement Park's massive billboard advertised the world's largest saltwater pool. New Yorkers flocked there in the summer months, even more so after the George Washington Bridge was finished in 1931.

But in the early 1900s the contrast between small-town, almost rural Fort Lee and the great metropolis across the river could not have been more stark than if the two had been separated by a continent. The city was visible from any number of vantages on the Jersey side, though in my father's own childhood all the tall buildings were below Canal Street—the great Woolworth skyscraper and other giants that were the world's marvels long before anybody had a notion to erect anything as ambitious as the Chrysler or Empire State buildings. To me those distant towers were just misty landmarks we happened to live near to like peasants in the shadows of the Himalayas, the famous skyline, like the great river below us, little more than scenic backdrops not unlike the ones we put together for our school theatricals.

My father was familiar from a young age with the Big City. After a year in that Carmelite seminary in Chicago, he spent a semester at

St. Francis Xavier Preparatory School on West 15th Street. He only attended long enough to learn the Greek alphabet, which he could still rattle off when I was memorizing it myself many years later. He was fourteen when he left school permanently, family finances requiring that he drop out of St. Francis and take a job. He found one as a courier working for a bank in the financial district and after that never willingly worked anywhere but Wall Street.

Other members of his generation preferred to work in or near Fort Lee. The film industry not only employed locals as assistant technicians, caterers and other hired hands, it spawned a lively support system of hotels, taverns and even luxury resorts, one right on the river itself, the other atop the Palisades with spectacular views of the river and Manhattan. I would come upon their ruins, as mysterious and to me as ancient as any Greek or Roman temples. Well into my adulthood Bill Miller's Riviera, a nightclub that boasted the biggest stars of comedy and popular music, was still open for business. Even further north yet another watering hole for the rich and famous, an edifice only slightly smaller than Buckingham Palace, remained intact. It later became an orphanage, then was turned back into a hotel.

When my parents could no longer afford to keep up the mortgage payments on the house on Center Avenue, we lived for a year in Englewood. Donald was already attending the Catholic high school there, though he would shortly leave for the seminary himself. We—my mother and father, Donald, my sister Rita who had already graduated high school—rented the second floor of a house just a couple blocks from St. Cecelia's, where I attended third grade. By then my father had managed to land a job at Bankers Trust on Wall Street, an entry-level position he would eventually parlay into department head. He got up even earlier than before and came home with regularity, with none of the after-work visits he used to make to bars on the way. He even managed to save enough money to buy a '39 Dodge.

Then, one evening my parents told me we would be moving back to Fort Lee the end of that same week. But it was only on the morning of the move that I was allowed to race around the neighborhood to say goodbye to friends. A year earlier we had moved from Fort Lee with the same suddenness, seemingly on the spur of the moment. I had barely managed to convince my parents to bring along a tank full of guppies Mariena had given me. They had bred prolifically with virtually no care and little food. As a last-minute concession someone put the tank into the trunk of our car. But no one thought to cover the tank, and by the time we reached Englewood it was dry and the guppies had disappeared.

Our new home in that garden apartment was in the rear of a building overlooking the back yards of some private homes on Hunter Avenue. A canopy of tall trees provided deep shade during much of the year. The rooms were new and modern. Until my brother Jack returned home from the Navy I had a bedroom to myself. My sister slept on a cot in the dining area. After Donald left the Army all six of us lived together again under one roof—for the last time.

Donald had gone straight from seminary to a recruiting office. Then he was back and forth on leave from one training camp or another. I don't remember there ever being a discussion, never mind controversy, about either of my brothers joining the service. The second world war had been over only half a decade and the draft was still in effect. Military service seemed a fate so obvious it didn't warrant discussion. Joining up was more honorable than waiting to be drafted—although of course my father never did either, though he supported my brothers' enlistments as if the military were a family tradition.

The day Donald left shipped out to Korea was the only time I ever saw my mother embrace anyone with that kind of feeling. My father and sister were at work that afternoon. Only my mother and I were there for the final goodbyes. Until the last moment she had seemed to have herself under control. There was a gentle hug, but then she suddenly flung her arms around his neck and pressed her mouth against his own. Donald assured her he would be back in eighteen months, calling her "Cookie," his pet name for her.

He looked very slim and handsome in his tan dress uniform. His fine blond hair had not yet thinned to the point of baldness as it would after months under a helmet. I don't know that he had had a real girlfriend yet. Throughout his life he remained fastidious about matters sexual. Once, Jack and he met near the naval base in Jacksonville and went to a nightclub. When the floor show came on and the young woman on stage began taking off her clothes, Donald quietly turned his chair around to avoid seeing her.

After he was wounded in Korea and was recuperating in Japan, he met a young Japanese woman with whom he had a relationship serious enough that his commanding officer and the company chaplain began writing letters to my parents. The letters suggested the young woman was not what she seemed to be but that Donald was too naif to realize it. Since then there has been a family joke about the possibility of a little Japanese-American that resulted from that relationship. But Donald was much too much of a gentleman not to have done the right thing if that had been the case.

When he was well enough for active duty he was sent to map roads in northern Japan. For six months he and a platoon of other men were off on their own in areas of the country only thinly unoccupied by the U.S. Army. As a result he learned Japanese as few American servicemen got the opportunity or the desire to do. He ate local cuisine and developed a deep appreciation for the nation and its people, an appreciation he maintained for the rest of his life.

I was also alone with my mother the day the telegram came informing her that Donald had been wounded. Just ten years old, being "wounded" did not seem to me a serious matter. It certainly wasn't when it happened to John Wayne or Alan Ladd. But my mother began weeping as if the telegram said Donald was dead. When Rita got home from work she told my mother that if his life were actually in danger they would not have sent a telegram until they saw whether or not he would survive. This may or may not have been true, but it helped calm my mother. At that point Rita was engaged to someone who was himself about to be drafted.

Later my mother said she had dreamed about Donald the night before she received the telegram, had seen him lying on a road in West Fort Lee where a car had hit him and his brother Jack when they were in elementary school.

It turned out his wound was indeed very serious. It took several months before he was well enough to be reassigned to duty. He tried to get himself assigned to combat duty, but the Army thought otherwise. That was how he ended up in the wilds of northern Japan, making maps and soaking up Japanese culture.

Shortly after Donald's return home a tempest was let loose upon the family. By then Jack had also been released from the service. No doubt the close confines of that apartment ignited my father's claustrophobia. I'm speculating, based on what he told me much later about how he had felt living in that apartment in the Bronx. Nor at the time did I understand the reasons for his resentment of his second son, that he was in fact in competition with Donald for his wife's affection. He could hardly confront such a situation the way he might an affection he suspected her of harboring for another man, a stranger like Matt Carson. He could not say to her: You love Donald more than you love me...than you ever loved me. The expression of such an accusation would be humiliating even to give voice to. And if he did, my mother would only deny it, proving nothing or, worse, might admit it.

I didn't know what words were exchanged behind the closed door of their bedroom or in later years when it was just the two of them sharing the same apartment. But I do know that whenever I saw my father tried to take her in his arms and profess his love for her, she always rebuffed him. What she actually felt must have been complicated and for that reason seem to her like something less than love, certainly less than what she felt for her favorite child. The sexual nature of her relationship with her husband also probably muddied the waters, making the love she did have for him seem less true, less "pure." Irish mothers are said to dote on their sons, idealize them, even feel something that verges on incest. But why her own feelings concentrated on Donald and not on one of his brothers or sister must have been as much a mystery to her as it was to anyone else.

The little boy who had jumped off her lap and told her he was *not* her little apple dumpling, must have come to reciprocate her special affection. And out of that they developed an understanding: He would rescue her from the man she was unhappily married to. And from the day that understanding was reached, whatever roof it was under which they lived could no longer be large enough to contain both Donald and his father. Father and son both knew it, though neither could admit what the real issue was. Instead, they waged a low-intensity war which after Donald's discharge broke out into nasty skirmishes, usually at the dinner table when my father was drinking and a non-family member such as Donald's fiancée was present.

The situation came to a head the first Thanksgiving after he returned home from the Far East. The entire family and guest were seated around the big maple table my parents had purchased the previous year on credit. My father was carving the turkey. Donald and his wife-to-be were seated side by side. Suddenly my father said something that caused Donald to stand up in his spotless tan uniform, a gold lieutenant's bar gleaming on each shoulder, and declare in a deep military voice, "I'm leaving this house and I'm never coming back!" He then stormed out of the apartment, followed by his older brother. Meanwhile my father continued carving, a drunken sneer on his face, having just destroyed the safe little world I inhabited as surely as if Joe Stalin had dropped an atom bomb on it.

Donald was taken in by his Uncle Pat who bought the house on Center Avenue we had owned until my father lost his job a few years earlier. Patrick was not really Donald's uncle. He was my mother's first cousin and as such was Donald's second cousin. My parents had sold Uncle Pat the house when they could no longer afford to make the mortgage payments. There might have been resentment on my father's part toward anyone who bought that house—the last my parents were to own—but the two families had ostensibly remained on good terms. My mother visited her cousin's wife on a regular basis. Patrick's daughter, my third cousin, was also my girlfriend and had been so since the day her family drove from the Bronx to have a look at the house with an eye toward buying it. So I went on spending a good deal of time there for my own reasons. I still got to visit those tall lilac bushes and sit in the big kitchen where my mother had cooked so many pot roasts and legs of lamb and had so many fights with my father.

Donald's moving in with Uncle Pat's family was a bitter pill for both his parents. For my mother it meant not only that he had turned his back on her for the sake of another woman, he was being supported in his treason by her own kin, the few members of her extended family with whom she had gotten on well. And if on some level my father was glad the young man who had monopolized so much of his wife's affection was now out of his house, any satisfaction on that account was counterbalanced by the resentment he bore toward his wife's cousin for having relieved him of his home and now his son as well.

DONALD
XIII

My name is Donald Francis Seiffert. I was born May 28, 1932.

I was the quiet one, the middle child. I left it to Rita and Jack to battle out who was going to be top dog. I followed them two and three years later through all the important milestones—first day of school, first communion, confirmation. The nuns in Madonna School knew who I was the first day of class before I had a chance to stand up like the others and tell them. "And you are Jack Seiffert's younger brother. But you won't be giving us the kind of trouble your brother did, will you," was the kind of encouraging start I began most school years. My sister was a model student, straight A's every semester in every class, but of course none of the teachers thought to compare me with her or assume I might follow her glorious record rather than Jack's. As a result I tried to cause more trouble in those classrooms than I ever really had an inclination to do. I didn't want to seem a wimp, unworthy of the name Seiffert which my brother had made notorious.

After elementary school it was another matter. Following his return from seminary, Jack attended a Catholic high school in New York for one year. When he was thrown out of there he went to Fort Lee High until he dropped out shortly before graduation. I started high school in Fort Lee High too but transferred in my sophomore year to St. Cecelia's in Englewood. I played on the football team in both schools, though I never gained the kind of glory my brother did. After junior year I entered a seminary in North Adams, Massachusetts. But I left in my senior year to joined the army and was sent to Korea after basic training. That was when I finally came into my own and was able to accomplish something outside my brother's shadow. At one point I was said to be the youngest sergeant in Korea. Shortly thereafter I received a battlefield commission and, who knows, probably would have made captain or even colonel if that gook hadn't sprayed me with his burp gun.

All this, of course, is history and water under the bridge. Now comes the part of my life where there seems to be a difference of opinion, mostly a difference between my opinion and everyone else's. To set the facts straight, I never got anyone pregnant in Japan or anyplace else. I never got anyone pregnant until I married my wife on March 15th, 1953. Even then, it was a full nine months until she delivered the baby. So, what happened between me and that young Japanese woman was purely something that was personal between the two of us. And that was how it should have remained, in my opinion, though my commanding officer and the chaplain and then my parents back in Fort Lee thought otherwise.

Contrary to what they all assumed, Yoshiko was not some floozy who picked me up in a bar or, worse, in one of those off-limits dives GIs were supposed to stay out of. It was me who did the picking up, improbable as it may seem given my tremendous shyness toward the opposite sex. But from the first time I laid eyes on her I never felt ill-at-ease when I was with Yoshiko.

She was standing on line waiting to buy food with the ration books that were still being issued to Japanese citizens by the government five years after the end of the war. A Japanese man, someone who looked the right age to have served in the Imperial Army, was having an argument with her. The Japanese are an orderly and well-behaved people, so that kind of scene was remarkable in itself. I assumed they were married or in some way related. But when I drew closer I realized the argument had started because the man tried to push his way into line ahead of her. My Japanese was good enough by then for me to make out most of what was being said.

Japanese war veterans generally kept a low profile when there were Americans around, but they assumed they should be paid special deference by their own people. I had no quarrel with the Japanese army (though after my return to the States I wasn't able to eat in a Chinese restaurant). At that point I wasn't especially attracted to the young woman. There were thousands like her on the streets of every Japanese city and small town, widows, mothers and sisters and children of the war dead. We were warned not to fraternize with them, though their need for basic necessities was so desperate many GIs flaunted regulations and did so anyway.

I pretty much kept to the letter of the law, but at that particular moment instinct took over—all those John Wayne movies, I guess—and I strode over to the line, inserted myself between the young woman and the man and demanded to see his identity papers. I was not an MP. There was nothing on my uniform to indicate I was. But wearing American fatigues in postwar Japan was all the authority you needed. The man was taken by surprise. He took a step back and inclined his head deferentially. But I could sense the hatred he felt at the sight of my uniform. He produced a small identity card that meant nothing to me, but I inspected it as if I knew what I was doing. I handed it back to him and told him in the best Japanese I could muster that if he continued to harass people I would see that he was put in jail. He put the card back in his pocket, bowed only as far he thought absolutely necessary and walked away.

This must sound like I was some kind of knight in shining armor. The truth is, I acted instinctively. The moment the man left I reverted to my usual shyness. But Yoshiko was not about to let me just walk away. She was only seventeen. She had lost her father and both brothers in the war and was caring for her mother and grandmother, trying to make do on the pittance allotted them by the government. If I had been in her shoes I think I would have hated the sight of anything American. But there was none of the bitterness I had detected in that Japanese man's eyes. Her big smile was open and full of warmth.

The first thing she did was compliment me on my Japanese. Then she said I must allow her to make me a meal in her mother's home. Even if she hadn't been as pretty as I then realized she was, I would have had a hard time resisting the temptation to eat a meal in a Japanese home. For the past six months I had been map-making in the northern parts of Hokkaido and had learned to appreciate some of the nuances of Japanese cuisine, a passion that has remained with me for the rest of my life. So, even though I was a stickler for the army regs and had punished many a grunt under my command for violating even minor ones, I accepted her invitation.

I'm not going to tell you I didn't fall in love with Yoshiko or even that we didn't have sexual relations. I did, and we did. I was still a virgin, if you can believe it—a twenty-year-old virgin who had spent more than two years in the United States Army and been exposed to more temptation than the average civilian sees in ten times that amount of time. Yoshie was almost as innocent as myself, though she was not a virgin, at least not technically, because she had been raped, first by Japanese soldiers when they were evacuating the city, then by at least one American during the early days of occupation. But I was the first man she had loved, she said, and I believed her. And she was certainly the first woman I had ever fallen in love with.

We spent all our free time together, which didn't actually amount to much because she was working sixteen and eighteen hours a day. At that point I had almost all my evenings free. She took me to parts of the city and suburbs few Americans got to see, oases of Japanese culture that showed what a premium they put on beauty and quiet. To me, it was as if she was showing me not parks and beautiful gardens but parts of her own interior landscape. She was small and slim, lively and energetic. She could walk the tail off me, and I had spent the last six months hiking fifteen miles a day with a full pack. But when she and I were sitting in one of those secluded gardens it was as if the peace of the place either entered into her or was there all along and she simply became in tune with it. Her eyes became as tranquil as the still water nearby. Holding the little hand that rested in my own in complete peace and trustfulness was like holding a water lily, cool, soft, weightless.

I don't mean to wax poetic. I'll leave that to my brother Tommy. I just want to make clear the kind of relationship I had with that young woman. I don't know where my commanding officer or the company chaplain got the idea there was something wrong or dangerous about it. Granted, the Army discouraged fraternization with the Japanese and only rarely consented to service personnel marrying them. Their reasoning was that American GIs were in an emotionally vulnerable state so many thousands of miles away from home and that they should remain faithful to their sweethearts and fiancées back in the States. This was true enough, as far as it goes. An eighteen-month tour of duty is a long time to spend in a foreign country. But I didn't have a sweetheart or fiancée back home. I was approaching my twentieth birthday and supposed to be able to make these kinds of decisions for myself. The young woman I was seeing was not alleged to be a member of any subversive or hostile organization. True, left to my own devices I might well have married her. But whose business was that?

What hurt most were the allegations that Yoshiko was an immoral woman who freely consorted with American GIs for money—a prostitute, in other words. I admit I was pretty naive in addition to being a virgin. But I don't believe for a moment anyone had evidence to substantiate that kind of accusation. I saw for myself how she earned her living, scrubbing pots and pans and performing other menial labor in local Japanese restaurants. Not that there weren't plenty of young women who *were* selling their bodies to Americans. But, given their economic situation, I felt I was in no position to judge them. The charges made against her by my CO and his chaplain were totally bogus. When they wrote to my parents telling them I had been taken in by a wily Japanese streetwalker, I saw red.

The day I received a letter from home (it was written in my father's hand but signed by both of them), repeating the lies they had been told, I stormed across the base to the CO's office. I barged past his secretary and, after pausing just long enough to throw a cursory salute, demanded to know why he was spreading evil slander about Yoshiko.

I could have been thrown in the brig for that kind of behavior. But the CO was a man who had seen combat both in Korea and in the South Pacific during the second world war. He knew from personal experience what I had been through. He was in his own way a stickler for rules and regulations, but he knew the difference between a real soldier and a pen-pusher with stars on his shoulders.

"With all due respect, sir, the Army has no business butting into my private life in this way. I haven't violated any Army regulations. I haven't compromised my duties in any way whatsoever."

He had been too stunned by my abrupt appearance to return my salute. He did so now and took a close look at me, probably to see if I was drunk. When he saw I was in command of my faculties, he told me to stand at ease. I snapped to, and while I waited for him to collect his thoughts I realized for the first time what I had just done. In the heat of battle I had frequently been the sole authority in command and I had exerted that authority fully. I tolerated no deviation from orders. When I met with resistance or cowardice I dealt with it promptly and vigorously. Even here in Japan, if someone had barged into my office and confronted me the way I had just confronted my CO, I would have put him in handcuffs. Instead, after first flushing crimson, he told me again to be "at ease," then invited me to sit down in the straight-back chair opposite his desk.

By that point I was trembling. In my mind I had acted much worse than I did in reality. It seemed to me I had spewed forth an angry ineffective full of insubordination. As I sat facing him, trying to keep my limbs under control, I tried to remember exactly what it was I had said. But all I could recall was a red blur as I stormed past the sergeant and then the shocked look on my commanding officer's face. I expected MPs to come through the door and put me in shackles. I thought if they did they would be entirely within their rights.

But the flush gradually faded from the CO's cheeks. He offered me a cigarette, sat back and crossed his legs. Then he called to his secretary, "Sergeant, you can close the door.

"How long have you been in country, Lieutenant?" he asked.

"Eighteen months, sir."

"And how much of that time in combat?"

"About eleven, sir."

"You spent two, three months in hospital, and another two or three recuperating. Then you were sent up north, if my memory serves."

"That's correct, sir."

"Which means you've only been down here in the big city for a couple, three months."

"Yes, sir."

"What I'm getting at, Lieutenant, is that after a year and a half of combat duty, followed by a lengthy hospitalization and then a tour of duty up in the sticks, you must still be adjusting to life on a base such as this well beyond the front lines. It must be pretty boring for you."

"Sir, I try to do my duty and follow orders," I replied like the young prig I was.

He sat studying me from his big wooden swivel chair as if I was presenting him with some kind of new life form he had never set eyes upon. "Lieutenant, you have a girl back home?"

"No, sir."

"Nobody special? Nobody you write to who's looking forward to your return?"

"No, sir," I said, the blood rushing to my own cheeks.

"But you have gone out with girls, of course. What I'm getting at," he said, squirming a bit, "this isn't the first time you've been with a woman."

To be honest, I didn't realize what he was meant. I was taking his words literally. "To be with a woman" I took to mean "to be in the company of a woman."

I told him, yes of course I had been, and was a bit surprised to see him nod in relief.

"Then, speaking man-to-man, I assume you're old enough to know there are women and...there are women."

Taking my silence for assent, he went on.

"These girls, I mean the sort of local girls you find in a situation like this, they have to look out for themselves. What I mean is, they're not exactly the sort of young women—the sort of young woman, I mean—we left behind in the States. I mean, if you *had* a girl back home.

"You see, Lieutenant, these girls had a pretty tough time of it during the war. Many of them lost most or all of their men folk. They have to get by as best they can. If they come across a GI who can help out, they owe it to their mothers and sisters to do what they can."

I still had no idea where he was going with this. His words seemed fashioned more to obscure his meaning than to reveal it. My father had a similar way of talking. He never gave me anything as formal or explicit as a "sex talk," but whenever he did refer to that subject he spoke in much the same confusing manner. But instead of breaking in and asking the CO a question that might clear up the situation I just listened quietly, pretending I understood what he was attempting so ineptly to say. I noticed he had stopped trying to make eye contact, as if it was he rather than myself who was guilty of a breach of conduct.

I had cooled down considerably. I no longer feared the MPs arriving any second to throw me into the brig. I even felt a glow of gratitude to the man on the other side of the desk (he seemed old enough to be my father, though he couldn't have been more than thirty-five). I had behaved in an unmilitary-like manner that boarded on insubordination, but he was treating me like a kindly uncle.

I never approached the chaplain about the matter. I assumed the clergy had a right to meddle in the sexual affairs of their flock. I didn't like it, I resented it, but I saw it as their merely doing their duty. Instead I blamed myself for having brought my behavior to the attention of the military authorities in the first place. As I lay on my bunk recalling what my commanding officer had said, it slowly dawned on me what he had been driving at. The idea that Yoshiko might have been using me had never for a moment crossed my mind. Nor did I believe it now. But something had changed in me. A seed of doubt had been planted. You have to remember, I was still a twenty-year-old with no experience of women. The only women I had been near on a regular basis were my mother and sister. My sister was capable of being mean to me, my mother might have punished me for something I didn't do. But neither of those relationships had given me any preparation for the kind of female my commanding officer was suggesting Yoshiko might be. Could I have been mistaken about her? I felt ashamed for even letting such a thought cross my mind, just as I had felt ashamed of myself so many times in the past for allowing "impure" thoughts to enter it. But, when those thoughts had occurred anyway, there was always the confessional to turn to. But who could I confess my treasonous doubts to about the woman I loved?

Yoshiko noticed the change in me and, putting two and two together, asked outright if I had been told the sorts of things that my CO had in fact had alleged. I denied everything like St. Peter in the garden when they took Christ away and asked Peter if he wasn't one of his disciples. When she saw that I wouldn't discuss the matter with her, she became angry and said me it would be better if we didn't see each other anymore. She said she didn't want to ruin my career, that she understood I was an American and she was Japanese and it probably never would have worked out anyway. She took all the blame on herself and even apologized in that way the Japanese have when there is absolutely no reason to apologize, when they are clearly in the right.

At that point I was in such a funk I scarcely put up any resistance. First my commanding officer, the representative of the organization to which I owed my complete loyalty, had told me in as fatherly way as possible that I was putting myself in grave personal and professional danger. Then the woman herself, speaking with as great or even greater authority as far as I was concerned precisely because she was a woman and because I loved her and because she was my first love and because I thought a woman must always be right in a situation like this, she seemed to be telling me that our relationship was wrong, if not morally wrong, then wrong for us, and wrong for me especially.

Afterward, I didn't allow myself to go into the kind of deep funk anyone would notice. I got up every morning and performed my duties like always. But in the evening I sometimes walked to one of the parks Yoshiko and I used to frequent, taking care not to choose one where I might run into her, and sat staring at the water lilies in a kind of shock, as if our breaking up had occurred just a few hours earlier. During the day I was alright, almost alright, my mind on my duties. But, come sunset, I lapsed into a state of numbness similar to what I had felt following my first experience of combat. Only, it went on day after day, week after week, until without my having noticed the passage of time I had to make a decision whether I would return to the United States or remain in Japan. Almost as soon as I was out of the anesthesia after my wounding I had put in for a new tour of duty in Korea. But the doctors now decided I was definitely no longer fit for combat. I loved Japan. I loved the Japanese people, their way of life, their food, the way they treated each other in hard times. Under other circumstances I might have decided to stay on or at least returned to that country after some time spent Stateside.

But nothing meant anything to me now. The entire Japanese nation was haunted for me by the ghost of one woman. I dreamed of and dreaded running into her on the street during my evening walks. I imagined reconciliations, recriminations, all sorts of scenarios. But mostly I dreaded seeing her, came to fear it as if there was something terrible I had done that I should be profoundly ashamed of. Looking back, I see there was. But I probably have blamed myself too much over the years, thinking I should have known better, that I should have seen through what was being done to me, that I should have trusted her and my feelings. Only now do I see I could not have acted any other way given my religious background, my innocence and my attitudes toward authority—just as it seems inconceivable I could have gone direct from seminary into a situation that required the killing of fellow human beings. I have to remind myself that in those days military service and Christianity did not present any contradiction. Didn't Cardinal Spelman go to Vietnam a few years later and tell the troops they were engaged in a holy war? What happened, happened. I dearly love the woman I eventually married who's given me five children. And my love of Japan did not die entirely, because for the rest of my life I have continued to read the history of that nation and even to become something of a Japanese chef—which has perhaps contributed to my being a bit overweight. But that's neither here nor there.

XIV

Sex is stronger than death. I didn't think of it that way when I was a child, but I can see that was a conclusion I inevitably had to come to. Certainly nothing was more important than sex in the world I lived in—at least not in the Roman Catholic world, which was almost all the world I knew despite living in a mainland state that was not very different in its habits and attitudes from a small town in Kansas. Nothing was more powerful than sex because sex not only equaled or surpassed every other human drive I was familiar with, it was the only force in the universe capable of standing up to and defying its almighty Ruler. Sex could send you to hell and eternal torment. It could drive you crazy with images of naked women—or at least what you imagined an image of a naked woman to be, something between what my mother looked like in a girdle and brassiere and the naked body of my doll Teresa who had no genital organs and only the slightest suggestion of nipples.

Sex—doing without it—was what turned otherwise normal human beings (and it was essential that we saw them as normal, not different from the rest of us, at least in their formative years) into priests and nuns thanks to a special calling by divine grace. And no-sex was not just a condition of the religious life, it was its very essence. Sex—not having anything to do with it outside the very strict limits set down by the church—pretty much contained the whole of the moral law and consequently preoccupied me day and night, worrying I would touch myself improperly, even inadvertently, or allow impure thoughts to enter my mind. Sex was the one topic my mother never talked about and, the single time my father did address the subject, made him stammer and blush. Sex was what Carol Miller did under viaducts with my best friend, Jimmy Dunn. Sex was dirty and disgusting and evil, like the slick kidney-shaped mud at the bottom of the stream that flowed beneath those viaducts, the nearby concrete covered with unfathomable graffiti and obscene drawings like primitive caves and grottoes given over to the celebration of an essential but forbidden human urge. Sex was bigger, more terrible than murder or war, more irresistible than lemon meringue pie.

I used to lie awake at night, thinking that if I were on my death bed mortality could not touch me as long as the woman of my desire still could. No disease or disability was that strong. So far, the only women I had actually touched in any way were my mother, my sister and a girlfriend who allowed me to hold her hand on special occasions. Even with that girl that much sex was exciting enough to cause me problems walking without exposing my arousal to the world.

Apart from talking back to my parents and "cursing," by which I meant four-letter words with which I and my friends peppered our conversation for the sake of seeming older than we were, the only offense I ever confessed was "impurity"—a word that could cover a multitude of sins, ranging from mass rape to the most innocent fantasy. I was guilty of neither offense, being incapable of even imagining rape, since I did not know what my penis was made for until I was well into my teenage years and had no accurate idea what a woman's body looked like until I was even older; and I never had any innocent sexual fantasies, since by definition all sexual thoughts were potential mortal sins. Yet I spent a good deal of my youth accumulating sexual sins to confess every two weeks and then being reprimanded by priests who rarely asked me to be more specific and assumed I was talking about masturbation or, as I grew older, something more adventurous. I didn't tell them my "impure thoughts" amounted to nothing more than a glance at the hind part of a cat or the glimpse of a brassiere ad in the *Ladies Home Journal.*

This was the same world in which my brothers and sister were raised. They, my brothers especially, experienced it no doubt in different ways than I did, partly because they escaped that world to some degree by attending public high school or because of the years they spent in the military (like myself, Rita went to Catholic schools from kindergarten through high school). But when Donald saw that young Japanese woman being abused by her male compatriot, he brought to that moment two decades of the kind of religious experience we all were exposed to, not to mention the drive, however damped down, that was the most powerful force in the universe after God himself. Combine that with the young Japanese woman's grateful smile and generous invitation to share a meal with her family, and tell me how any man could resist.

Repeat the same scene under different circumstances a year later after he had returned home a war hero to small-town New Jersey. He's in a tavern in Coytesville, the land of thespian orgies four decades earlier, perhaps the same tavern where Theda Bara and John Barrymore cavorted to the fascination and horror of every upstanding mother in Fort Lee proper. By now it was just a rundown bar, a place to meet old friends from his year spent in Fort Lee High. Enter that same Japanese bully in the form of a former halfback who played on the same football team with Donald until Donald was diagnosed, incorrectly, as having a heart murmur. The bully begins harassing a former classmate, a pretty girl also with a nice smile. Donald steps forward and in the unnaturally deep voice he has acquired from three years of barking commands grabs the former halfback by the shirtfront and pushes him against the bar. "You can leave on your own, or we can step outside." It's a line worthy of a William Holden or Gary Cooper, and that young woman—my brother's future wife—knows it.

This was the beginning of an episode that prompted many long discussions between my parents and our parish curate across our big dining table: two young people drawn to each other by way of a movie scene they had both witnessed too many times not to respond to when they came upon it in real life. And it was indeed sex, but not in the narrow sense that priest and my parents thought, whatever it was those two young people were up to after the young woman's parents had gone to bed for the night. It was SEX. But my mother could not admit there was anything more to it than temptation and sin: a young woman using her physical charms on an inexperienced young man who happened to be my mother's favorite child.

SEX was also what drove my father to abuse his son at the dinner table that terrible Thanksgiving afternoon. SEX was why Donald had to announce he was leaving that house and never coming back. SEX was what drove my sister to hysterics and made her lock herself in the bathroom after my father said he was going to speak to her young man about his "intentions." SEX was the force that would save me from death no matter how ill I was, the one power in creation capable of resisting the fate everyone, saved and condemned, had to face. SEX was everything God himself was: imminent, omnipotent, irresistible and, at least for the uninitiated like myself, unimaginable. We humans were steeped in it, obsessed with it, terrified of it, guilty of it.

Looking back, it's easy to think what a waste of energy went into all that repression and anxiety and how distorted our notion of sex was. But I think in some ways we actually had it right. Sex actually is everything, and was so long before Dr. Freud discovered it, which is why we were taught to see him, along with Karl Marx, as more evil than Adolf Hitler, because Freud had latched onto something more essential and more dangerous than Hitler (what went on in the Nazi extermination camps back then was still just a detail of the recent war). But it would be a long time before I came to understand the issue was not so much a matter of accepting or rejecting sex, embracing or shunning it as the ultimate trap set for us by the Devil, as it was a question of accepting sex as the essence of life itself.

Psychologists say no one is oversexed, but surely some are more closely in touch with their sexual natures and more driven by them than are other people. It seems ironic that I and my brothers and sister all had powerful sex drives and yet we all aspired to states that required celibacy – perhaps for the very reason that those drives were so powerful. In such an environment we saw ourselves as not so much unsuited for the religious life as we were like the rich who have so much more to give and hence give up to their poorer brethren. Never mind the impossibility of trying to stuff that powerful genie into a bottle or the psychic consequences of trying to do so during the years that are so critical to someone's development. Never mind centuries of Irish Jansenism, Bavarian puritanism and American Victorian sexual attitudes. We were dealing with something more seismic than repression, something stronger than social mores or even than morality itself.

MARY

XIV

I've tried to love each of my children equally. I know all parents say that, and most mean it. But the truth is it isn't possible, you always love one more than the other, or at least you find something about one of them that appeals to you in a way you can't put your finger on, even if it makes you feel guilty.

In my case it was Donald. Which is odd, because he was the one child who didn't seem to want my attention, at least beyond a certain point. When he was small I used to sit him on my lap and call him my apple dumpling. Then, one day, he couldn't have been more than two or three at the time, he looked up and said, "I'm not you're apple dumpling!" and jumped off my lap. That's enough to break your heart, I can tell you, after you've borne and nursed a child and loved him more than you do your own flesh.

As a little boy, all he would eat was peanut-butter-and-jelly sandwiches and milk. He refused to eat vegetables at all and didn't seem to care for meat, not even franks and hamburgers, which the other kids gobbled up like horses, though during the war meat was scarce even with John bringing home what he could from the butcher shop. He, Donald, stayed skinny as a rail, and every time he got sick I prayed to God He wouldn't take him, he'd get such big dark rings under his eyes. It was Rita, and later Tommy, who came down with scarlet fever without either of the older boys catching it. But Donald looked like he was at death's door if he just had the sniffles.

I've read in women's magazines that a mother can become too closely attached to her children, especially her male children, when her husband isn't giving her enough attention or she feels frustrated in her marriage for some other reason. God knows I wasn't getting the attention I craved during those days on Cumley Terrace, what with John gallivanting in New York and away sometimes for days at a time. I was a city girl and wasn't used to the quiet, never mind the isolation, all by myself in a house with three children to look after, and then a new baby when Tommy came along. I was used to being able to walk out my front door and onto Fifth Avenue in Manhattan or Adrian Avenue in the Bronx where my mother's house was located. In the city I had the sense of never really being alone. I could stroll over to Van Cortlandt Park with one of the kids in a baby carriage and the others trailing along beside me, and I may as well have been in the country upstate, it was so green and peaceful. And if I wanted to get back into city life again all I had to do was walk over to Broadway.

In Fort Lee—Leonia, actually, we were just outside the city limits of Fort Lee—it was another story. The women on that block only seemed to come out of their houses to hang out wash or go down to the supermarket with their husbands. That was another thing—we didn't own a car. John had to sell his Dodge after the Crash, and we didn't get another until after the war when he bought a 1939 Dodge. So, there I was stuck in that house with three children and no husband half the time. It's a wonder I didn't go bonkers. Sometimes John's relatives visited, even when he was away on one one of his toots. His sister Francie especially. She's still a friend to me, calls me up even though we're both now into our eighties. I forget exactly how old I am, to tell you the truth, I can barely remember what I had for breakfast this morning. But, for some reason what happened fifty, sixty, even seventy years ago is still clear as day. It's as if by forgetting what happened yesterday or ten years ago, I've cleared the decks inside my memory so I can better remember what happened way back then.

Anyway, there I was with three small children, and they were all I had to love because even when John was home he was so full of beer he wasn't much good for anything but sleeping it off. I was a young woman with a young woman's appetites, and though at the time I thought all I could do was suffer through it and offer it up for the suffering souls in purgatory, I knew my youth was being wasted. If I saw a good-looking garbage man the thought would cross my mind, There's a fellow I

wouldn't mind his leaving his shoes under my bed. I'd immediately
chalk it up as a sin and tell it the next time I went to confession, though
God knows I was terrified of Father Corcoran, though he never raised
his voice to me in the confessional the way he did with other people.
I used to sit in the pew waiting my turn, and sure as shootin' a couple
minutes after someone went into the box you'd hear Corcoran's voice
get louder and louder until those of us waiting for our confessions to
be heard would start to sweat, thinking this was what was in store for
us too. You could hear every word he said. What you couldn't hear was
the voice of the person confessing. It was like listening to one side of
a telephone conversation. "You did what?! How many times?!" By the
time it was my turn I was sick to my stomach.

But, as I say, he was always gentle and soft-spoken with me and
outside the confessional Corcoran could be a charming man. We didn't
live that far from the church grounds situated atop a little hill
overlooking the cemetery. Sometimes of an afternoon I would walk
up to make a visit to the Blessed Sacrament. Usually there was no one
inside the cool dark church. Even on a hot summer afternoon it was
always pleasant in there and smelled the way churches did back in the
Bronx. On the left side of the main altar was a statue of the Blessed
Mother, and on the right was one of St. Joseph, her foster husband. The
lights were all out in the daytime when there was no service in progress.
But the red vigil lamp was always burning next to the tabernacle, and
usually there was a spotlight left on over the altar itself. Even so, it took
a while for your eyes to become accustomed to the dark, especially on
a bright afternoon. I didn't stay long. I never had more than fifteen
minutes or half an hour to myself. Maybe it was Francie who was
watching the kids or, more likely, I left Rita in charge. I just needed to
get away for a few minutes, and where else could I go? There was hardly
a store of any kind within walking distance. We were situated on the
back edge of the Hudson Palisades. I could walk down Fort Lee Road
to the shopping area of Leonia without any trouble, but it was a long

trek back and all steeply uphill. So if I wanted to get away by myself for a few minutes the church was the handiest thing I had. Besides, it was a lovely view from there, though cold as the dickens in winter. But I'll never forget the gorgeous summer afternoons, with that long view to the west all the way to the mountains—I don't even know the name of them – in the western part of the state or maybe it was Pennsylvania. And the great valley in between. The sunsets were spectacular, even better than they were from our back yard.

Sometimes when I was coming out of church I would run into Father Corcoran. He liked to stroll around the grounds reading his office—all priests had to complete it before midnight under pain of mortal sin. He would be wearing his black cassock, walking slowly up and down the macadam drive only funeral cars were allowed to use, ordinary automobiles had to park in the dirt lot nearby. He was a man in his mid-forties at that time, but he was mostly bald and much of the hair he had left was white. He wasn't terribly tall, and he had the complexion of a boiled lobster, with two small green eyes and large pink lips, the thickest lips I've ever seen on an Irishman. And a brogue you could cut with a knife. Even so, he wasn't a bad-looking man, though to me of course he was always a priest, and my parish priest to boot, not to mention my confessor. He knew very well who it was kneeling there when he pushed the slide back in the confessional and I began my, "Bless me father for I have sinned, it is two weeks since my last confession..." It was he I had to confess those impure thoughts I had about the garbage man and other notions I got when John was away or was too drunk even to carry on a conversation and I was left all alone with three children, a young woman with a young woman's appetites.

Although Corcoran never raised his voice to me in the confessional, I still trembled when I pushed back the heavy maroon curtain and entered the dark booth and saw his profile outlined in the darkness. Each time I expected him to explode, which would have been bad enough for my nerves, but it was the other people still waiting to have their confessions heard I was mostly concerned about. How could I face them if he bellowed out to me as he did to so many others, "You did what? How many times, you say?!" I'd be too ashamed to go to Sunday mass for fear of running into any of those people, for God knows what they would have made of what he had said. No doubt their imaginations would run wild, just as my own did when it was me kneeling in the pews waiting my turn.

But all he ever said after I confessed was, "For your penance say five Our Fathers and five Hail Marys." And then he'd incline his big white head toward the screen separating us and whisper, "And say a prayer for me." I knew from overhearing other people's confessions—I mean, from overhearing the priest when they were in there confessing—that the other penances he doled out were much stiffer, a couple of rosaries or even a series of visits to the Blessed Sacrament. But, of course, if he also whispered it to them the way he did to me I don't know if he also asked them to say a prayer for him.

I didn't know what to make of that request, just as I didn't know what to make of his never raising his voice. And, to top it all off, whenever I ran into him during those visits I made to the church of an afternoon when I just couldn't take it anymore back at the house, if he chanced to notice me at all when he was deep into his office he never failed to show a pleasant smile and offer his small hand, which never really gripped my own but just sort of lay in it for a few seconds the way a woman might shake hands.

"How are you, Mary?" he said. I blushed not just because a priest was calling me by my first name—what else would he call me?—but because I couldn't imagine he didn't remember I was the one who had those evil thoughts about the garbage man.

He would ask about my children and, after I brought my mother over to live with us, about her as well. He was almost my parents' contemporary and a fellow countryman, though from Tipperary, which is some out of the way place in the old country. My people were from Kerry. But, of course he and my parents were all exiles now in a foreign land. So whenever he ran into me he asked about them, and sometimes he would even turn up in our front yard for a visit. My mother got on well with Corcoran, much better than I did because I could never get over my fear of him. Mom was never daunted by the clergy. In fact, I can never remember her having a good word to say about them. In that respect she was as different from the Seifferts as people of the same religion could possibly be. She enjoyed Corcoran's company as a fellow Irishman, not because he was clergy. And sometimes my father and Corcoran would sit on lawn chairs in the front yard and smoke cigars or sip iced tea or lemonade and even occasionally a cold beer. At those times I felt like I was a kid again. All I could do was make sure they all had whatever they wanted to eat or drink and keep an eye on the kids at the same time.

But I was talking about Donald, wasn't I.

A mother's feelings toward her child are complicated. As a woman you can love a man with all your heart and all your strength and all your will, but if he does something to weaken or destroy that love, you can never get it back. With a child, it's another matter. He's yours, he's part of you, and nothing he does or says can fundamentally change your feelings toward him.

So, when my "little apple dumpling" jumped off my lap that day and told me he was no such thing, he might have broken my heart but he didn't kill my love for him. If anything, I felt it more strongly. For a brief moment I hated him, it was a shock coming like that so unexpectedly. Whenever his older brother sat on my lap, at least until he was a couple years old, he sat there happily because it was in expectation of nursing from me. After he had his fill he fell right asleep, and to this day he seems to sleep at least as much as he's awake. But, after feeding, Donald would lie wide-awake gazing up at me as if he knew exactly what I was thinking. What I was thinking was how much I loved him, how frighteningly much I loved him. I used to wonder why I hadn't felt this kind of intensity towards my first two, but I never could come up with any explanation.

Donald has gray-blue eyes, the same as myself, and he's nearsighted and damn near blind in one of them, just like me as well. But of course I couldn't know that would be the case, not back when he was just a little one. It was something behind those eyes that held me and, for the life of me, if I sat here for another ten years I don't think I'd be able to explain why it was so. Why do we love one person far and away above what we feel for others? If it was out of frustration because my husband was running around and paying very little attention to me, why didn't I feel the same thing for the boy's older brother or sister, or even for the baby I had a few years later?

You might think I indulged Donald as a result of the special feelings I had for him. But the truth is I went out of my way not to, though he seemed to know I wanted to and that in a crunch I couldn't say no to him as long as I could justify to myself that what I was doing was not showing favoritism. I thought it would be a sin to act as if I loved him better than his brothers and sister. Not one of those sins in the catalog you went through when you are examining your conscience before confession—the ten Commandments, missing mass on Sunday, having impure thoughts—but a sin nonetheless, a failure as a parent in her duty not to show preference for one child over another. But it never occurred to me to feel guilty about how I actually felt toward him. That's the advantage of being a woman, I suppose. We can't help what we feel. If there was love in my heart, how could that be sinful? It would only be a sin if I did the wrong thing, if I acted on it in the wrong way, just as if I felt something for a man who is not my husband and entertained impure thoughts about it, the way I did about that garbage man, though "entertained" would be an exaggeration. The thoughts came unannounced, and God knows I tried to flush them out as fast as they came, but sometimes I couldn't, I was so hard up and so lonely.

Anyways, I treated Donald the same as I did my other children, and ninety-nine percent of the time I believed I didn't feel anything for him I didn't also feel for his brothers and sister. But then something would happen to remind me this wasn't so, such as the time he and Jack got hit by a car.

They were on their way to school at the other end of town. It was an early spring morning, I remember thinking it would be a good day to plant some green beans. It was a great moment for me when the three of them were packed off to school and I had the rest of the day to myself, till three o'clock, at least. To see me then you might think I was a happy woman, singing as I hung the wash out and swept off the bit of patio behind the house. At such times I could think to myself, my lot isn't so bad after all, I could have it worse. I had three healthy children and a little house of my own, and please God if my husband would only stop drinking and gallivanting, what right would I have to complain about anything at all?

That was when the police car pulled up. I had seen it cruising down the block when I was inspecting the rosebushes for Japanese beetles. The beetles were a great menace and we fought them all summer long, picking them off the roses by hand and burning them in pots. At first I thought someone must have taken sick in the neighborhood—there were a number of old people on the block. But then I thought to myself, no, it would be an ambulance in that case, not a police car. But then the car pulled up to the curb, and the cop, not an old man but he already had a wad of fat hanging over his belt—you'd never see that sort of thing on a policeman in New York, at least not on someone his age. I knew immediately something had happened. My knees grew weak and the pruning shears suddenly became so heavy I didn't think I could hold them any longer.

"Mrs. Seiffert," he says.

"Yes," I say.

"I'm afraid there's been an accident."

My heart dropped, it literally felt as if it stopped beating. "Jesus, Mary and Joseph."

"They've been taken to the hospital. I can drive you there."

I knew it must be Donald who was hurt bad because if it wasn't I wouldn't be feeling as terrible as I did. That sounds awful, I know, as if I wouldn't have cared if it had been Jack or Rita. Of course I would. But it would have been different.

I was shaking so bad when I got into the patrol car I didn't even think to ask where we were going.

"Is he bad?" I said when I could manage to speak.

"They're both still in the emergency room," he said. "One of them got knocked over, but there are tire marks on the shirt of the other."

Nowadays a cop would never tell you something like that. Back then they thought they were doing their duty, giving you a full report even if it meant filling in the gory details. Doctors were the same way. But that cop didn't have to tell me which of them had the tire marks across his chest, that chest I used to hold so close I could feel his little heart beating against mine. I didn't try to say anything else until we reached the emergency room at Englewood Hospital, that was where they had brought the two of them. The nurses tried to keep me from going in, but I pushed my way past until I found the two of them lying behind a green curtain with a nurse fussing over Jack and a young doctor, an intern I suppose, taking Donald's blood pressure. When I saw he was conscious and he seemed to recognize me, the tight spring inside my chest snapped and I started to ball like a kid. Even at the age of eight he was still such a tiny thing, so slight and pale, while his older brother had always been stocky and for that reason looked as if he was able to take care of himself even as he lay on that cot in the emergency room with God-knew what kind of injuries.

I forced myself to go to Jack's bedside first.

"It was his idea, Mom," he said. "He said if we ran we could make it. I told him to wait, but he went ahead anyway."

"And of course like an idiot you followed him."

I turned toward his brother then, looking for the tire marks, though his chest was covered with a starched white sheet.

"And you? What have you got to say for yourself?"

He looked up at me with those gray-blue eyes just the same as he used to when he was a baby lying on my lap, only now there was something in them that was more fathomable, less mysterious, but still challenging. It was as if he were throwing my own words back at me, as if what had happened that morning had been deliberate and of his choosing. To spite me. There I was, scared to death I'd find him dead or dying or permanently crippled. And then I find somehow he has miraculously escaped serious injury—to this day no one can explain how those tire marks could have got on his chest and he wasn't crushed— and after all he's put me through he looks up as if to say, "I'm still not your apple dumpling."

I could have clouted him.

The upshot was he had a broken leg in a cast and that kept him home from school for the next three months. But every day I gave thanks to God, it could have been so much worse. Of course the other two, especially Jack, were annoyed Donald got to stay out of school for a full semester and they didn't.

So, there we were, the two of us, with me waiting on him hand and foot. Angry as I was for his running out in front of that car, I felt somehow it was my fault he had done so because I imagined he did it to hurt me. I couldn't think why, but it seemed of a piece with his jumping off my lap and telling me he was not my apple dumpling, that and the look in his eyes in the emergency room.

I felt the same way when my little sister died, as if I had done something wrong, as if the least I could have done was die with her. I had always been the one responsible for her. It was me who walked her to school on her first day and dressed her for her first communion. But, unlike the way I felt toward my other sister, Anna, I never resented having to look after Elizabeth. Apart from my oldest brother Marty, Elizabeth was the one I loved best in the family, maybe the only one I truly loved. There were two years between us, but we could sit and talk as if we were the same age. We both had notions about getting an education—which in those days meant high school—and marrying men with good futures, men who didn't drink or run around the way our father and older brothers did. We weren't going to be like our mother, beaten down, a drudge and slave to her children and ne'er-do-well husband.

This was a revolutionary time for women in America, you have to remember, and even as kids we felt it. In just a couple years women would get the vote, and before long they would be cutting off their long hair which required so much time and attention, "one hundred strokes a night," and throwing out their corsets—my mother never came down to breakfast in the morning without first putting on her corset. Elizabeth and I anticipated all of this because it was in the air around us, even on Adrian Avenue. If you saw the two of us in a photograph you could easily mistake us for twins, though of course she was a few inches shorter.

And then overnight she seemed to go from being a healthy, frolicsome kid to a very sick one. We all knew about tuberculosis. It seemed just about every family had someone with TB. It was like AIDS, only more so, because it was more widespread and because there didn't seem to be anything you could do to avoid it and because it struck down children as well as adults. The only other disease I can compare it to it is polio back before vaccines were invented and you lived in dread if your child went to a swimming pool for fear he would pick up something in the water. One of Rita's best friends came down with polio and spent her entire life in one of those rocking beds, otherwise she couldn't breathe. She was one of the lucky ones because she didn't die outright or end up in an iron lung. That was how bad TB was. You prayed to God you or someone near to you wouldn't get it, but you knew it was out there and you lived in its shadow, even children.

But it seemed especially cruel to me when it struck down Elizabeth. If it had been my mother or my father or anybody except maybe Marty, I could have taken it somehow in stride as God's will. But Elizabeth was the dearest thing to me in the entire world, and I couldn't imagine Him inflicting her with such a curse without my being somehow responsible. It was as if her getting TB was the price of my love, that somehow you ran the risk of killing someone by loving them so much. As a kid I didn't think any of this through the way I'm doing now, but I felt it nonetheless, just as I felt it when Donald got hit by that car. It's a terrible thing to believe your love can kill someone.

Anyway, I had to watch her wither away and then see them take her out of the house in one of those meat wagons they called ambulances. I hadn't the foggiest notion where Governors Island was, only that it was far away and you had to take a boat to get there. I only saw her once in that hospital, just before she died. I hardly recognized her, she was so thin, her gray-blue eyes swollen all out of proportion to the rest of her face. I sat beside her bed and held her little hand until my mother said it was time to go and we kissed her, and that was the last time I saw her alive.

Is it any wonder I felt the way I did when Donald narrowly escaped being killed by that car? I never thought for a moment it didn't actually run him over. His surviving was a miracle pure and simple. God had spared him, and now it was up to me to nurse him back to health, preserve him for whatever it was God had in mind for him. Maybe, I even thought, that was why the child had spurned me, because he sensed even as a toddler he was destined for something greater than human love, that God Almighty had chosen him in a special way to fulfill His will.

Throughout his recuperation I pampered him, offered to cook whatever he liked, though he still preferred peanut-butter-and-jelly sandwiches to anything else. I read to him out of our set of *Journeys Through Bookland*. I let him listen to his favorite radio programs even when it was past his bedtime and the other children were asleep. Of course, I also made sure he kept up with school lessons the other two brought home for him each day.

When the cast finally came off I was of two minds, happy he was recovering but anticipating the loss I would feel when he was no longer with me all day. If there was ever a time we could be said to have grown close, I mean once he was no longer an infant, it was during those three months. He never relented to the point of letting me caress him or call him my little apple dumpling or anything of the kind, but of necessity he was obliged to let me take care of him physically, almost as if he were a young child again. I can't say he enjoyed it, but he never complained and if after washing him or cutting his hair I planted a kiss on his forehead, sometimes he looked up at me with something less than disdain and his lips almost bent into a smile. That was enough for me. That made my heart overflow.

RITA
XV

My name is Rita Mary Seiffert Cabrini. I was born June 4th, 1930. I graduated from the Academy of the Holy Angels June 23rd, 1948. I was married January 10th, 1954 to Robert Edward Cabrini. We've had eight children of our own and have adopted three others. My first pregnancy was twins, but the little girl died the day after she was born. I have been a lifelong Roman Catholic and have raised all my children to be Catholics, though you wouldn't know it today if you knew some of them. I believe in God. I believe that Jesus Christ is the Son of God and that He died on the cross for our sins. I believe that He will sit in judgment on the living and the dead, and I hope and pray to be among those who will be admitted to paradise.

Religion has always been important to me. You could say it's the most important thing in my life. When I was a teenager I toyed with the idea of becoming a nun — "toyed" is not the right word, because I took the matter very seriously — but in the end I decided I could do God's will better by raising a family of my own. I always wanted to have a family, and a big one at that. I wanted twelve children, an even dozen, like in the movie *Cheaper by the Dozen*. I don't know how many times I've seen that film, I still love it. Anyway, I made no bones about what I wanted and Bobby, my then-future husband, he raised no objection. I can complain of other things about the man, but one thing I have to grant him is that he enjoyed having a family as much as I did.

Given my ambition you would think I married early like my mother. But the truth is I didn't get married till I was twenty-three, which was pretty late for my generation. We had to wait till Bobby got out of the service—he was drafted during the Korean War. And then for some reason I had trouble getting pregnant with the first child, with the twins I mean. None of my pregnancies was easy and I lost a few to miscarriages along the way. But that was God's will.

People thought I was crazy, having that many children. Mostly they assumed it was because I was Catholic and wasn't allowed to practice birth control. But birth control had nothing to do with it. As I said, I wanted twelve children, and if my insides didn't give out after the eighth baby I would have. As it is, I love the three Koreans I adopted as much as if they were my own. But I took a lot of heat from people along the way. There was one nosy neighbor when we lived in Dumont who confronted me practically every day across the driveway about how could I go on having children when there were so many people in the world already and there wasn't enough food to feed them. I think I held my own in those discussions. I was even grateful for them, because talking helped make clear in my mind what I already believed. At the time I only had four.

She was some kind of protestant, I forget which denomination, and had just two children of her own and lost one of them to a car accident when he was twenty or twenty-one years old. You would think losing a child would make her see the value in having a bunch of kids if only as a hedge against finding herself childless in her old age. But she was violently pro-birth control, and she assumed it was because I was Catholic that I was having a child more or less every other year. No matter how much I told her it was because I loved children and because I believed each child was a gift from God, she never seemed willing to take me at my word and never softened her argument by one scintilla. Even so, I enjoyed our discussions.

Despite having the kids around me all the time, especially when they were young, it was a long day in that big house all by myself while my husband was at work. At the time, my mother was still living in Fort Lee and neither of us had a driver's license. Sometimes she took the 86 bus to visit me during the week, but I couldn't travel so easily. When she did pay a visit her attitude wasn't always what you would call positive. She had her own ideas about child-rearing, and they didn't precisely coincide with my own. I loved my mother very much, but I can't say I always had the feeling she responded the same way toward me. She doted on my brothers like every Irish mother, but when it came to her daughter there was always something that needed to be reformed or whipped into shape. She even criticized the way I went around the house in an old house dress, though there was no one there but myself and the children. But that's the kind of woman she was, and I'd just as soon not get into that subject.

My husband and I were happy. Previously we had lived in apartments, which was all well and good until the third child came along. Then we needed the extra room, and that was when we bought the house in Dumont. Later we had to move to an even larger house, in Plainfield. I hated leaving Dumont. Even though we sold the place to my parents and the property remained in the family and I could go back to visit anytime I wanted (I never did), I cried something awful the day we moved. We were very happy there.

Sometimes I wonder what my life would have been like if we had stopped having children at that point and settled for four, as my mother and father had done, and not moved. Nowadays no one would question someone having just two or three children even if they're a practicing Catholic. But back then I would have had to get special permission to practice the rhythm method, though some of my friends were already using contraceptives and the priest was telling them in the confessional it was okay. That's something I could never understand. Either something is right or it's wrong. How can the pope say one thing and the priest in a confessional allow a penitent to act contrary to what the pope has decreed? I could no more use contraceptives than I could get an abortion. Either one is a mortal sin, though I don't believe using a condom is the same as taking a child from a mother's womb. I'm not a fanatic, I just don't understand today's Catholics, as if it were up to them what they believe or do not believe.

But I started writing this so I could put my two cents in about what everyone else has been talking about—the time when Donald returned from Korea and we were all living in that garden apartment on Center Avenue. My husband-to-be, as I say, was still in the army, stationed in Texas. We hadn't been dating very long before he was drafted, but I was very much in love. Which came as much as a surprise to me as it did to people who knew me because for many years before that I had expected to marry Tim McCullough. Tim had taken me to my high school prom and we had been dating since I was sixteen. He was drafted himself, into the Air Force, and shipped out just a few months before I met Bobby. The day I said goodbye to Tim I felt as if he was taking my heart with him. I actually had chest pains. My mother insisted I see a doctor—there's plenty of heart trouble on her side of the family. I cried for days after Tim left. Even after I was married I still carried his picture in my wallet.

Anyway, that was the situation when Donald was discharged from the Army and lived with us briefly in that four-and-a-half-room apartment. Jack had gotten out of the Navy not long before. Before that it had been just my mother and father, me and my baby brother Tommy. I slept in a little alcove off the dining room. When Jack came home from the Navy he shared one of the bedrooms with Tommy. When Donald returned from Korea, a war hero with medals all over his chest, my parents bought a sofa bed for him to sleep on. It was pretty crowded, but I, for one, didn't mind. I was happy to have us all under the same roof again, especially to have my brother Jack in the house again.

But of course there was no accounting for my father. He had treated both the boys harshly when they were young (Tommy was another matter, I don't think he ever laid a hand on him and he was spoiled rotten). Jack and Donald were grown men now, but even so. It had been such a close call for Donald in Korea, he might easily have come home in a coffin. Pop must have decided to cut him some slack—until that scene at Thanksgiving dinner when Donald walked out and never came back.

At the time I thought it was Donald's fault. Not that I was one to take my father's side. What I felt toward him in those days was something close to hatred, though for the life of me I don't know what it was he did that should have made me feel that way. I think it was because I was still so much my mother's daughter, I wanted her approval so badly. And she held the man in such contempt, I couldn't help but take my cue from her. Now when I look back on some of the things I did I feel ashamed. I actually slapped his face once. Later I tried to make it up to him, after I was married and the children began to come. I always asked after him and tried to treat him well when he came to my house to visit.

But, little did I know there was something going on in that house besides Donald's feud with my father. We all knew my brother Jack was a lady's man, girls had been hanging on him ever since he was able to walk. There was one who used to try to pull him through the fence in our backyard on Cumley Place. She would lure him with the promise of candy or a piece of the cupcakes she seemed to have an endless supply of. I warned Jack to stay away from her, but he could never pass up a sweet. Sure enough, once he came within reach she latched onto him and held him against the fence, kissing him over and over while he stood munching a devil- food cupcake or calmly unwrapping a piece of rock candy she had given him. I was hysterical, thinking she meant to hurt or even kidnap him, the way my mother told us we should be wary of strangers giving us candy to lure us into their cars. But Jack was either too stupid or didn't care, so I had to take matters in my own hands, and that meant pummeling the girl until she let go of him. But the next day it would be the same thing all over again, he never learned.

That was pretty much the story of his life, at least when it came to the opposite sex. When we started grammar school—I was a year behind him—he always had two or three girls vying for his attention in the schoolyard when he was playing punch ball. He pretended not to notice, but after school he would let one of them carry his books for him and they would fight among themselves over who got the privilege. Even the nuns were sweet on him. He got away with murder as a result, and of course he loved being the center of attention. I think that was the real reason why he became an altar boy, so everyone could see him out there in front of the congregation, the only other competition being the priest himself. When he was older he used to act as master of ceremonies at high masses on Christmas and Easter and served more than his share of funerals and weddings.

From the time we were little kids he said he was going to become a priest. I always thought he would do so and would make a good one, one of those priests everyone loved, whose attention they fought for, just as those girls fought over him in the schoolyard. It never occurred to me there would be any conflict between his appetite for the opposite sex and his vocation. It probably didn't occur to him either, or at least not seriously so, until he went away to a junior seminary in Ohio. I never got a single letter from him throughout the year he was there. Donald got two, but Donald was also thinking of going into the priesthood. I suppose those letters were by way of epistles from the front lines, male stuff. My parents received the requisite note from him every month— the priests insisted all the boys write their parents on a regular basis as if they were away at summer camp.

When Jack came back from seminary he seemed changed. He was about to turn fifteen, myself fourteen. He had shot up about three inches during the year he was away and seemed even better looking than he had before. My parents put him into Cardinal Hayes High School in New York City—it was no worse a trip traveling to the Bronx then it was to the nearest Catholic high school in New Jersey. Cardinal Hayes was an all-boys school taught by Christian Brothers who had a reputation for being strict disciplinarians. My brother had never been exposed to much in the way of male discipline before that, with the exception of our father whose discipline was closer to brutality than correction. But the Brothers would stand for no nonsense, and Jack was just the kind of kid they liked to get their hands on and whip into shape. Only, he would have none of it. He came home with bruises or even a black eye, but went back the next day and gave them the same lip all over again. Of course, my parents, like all Catholics of their generation, approved physical punishment when it was administered by the clergy. They figured Jack was a wild kid who needed a strong hand. But it didn't work, and eventually the Brothers gave up and expelled him. After that there was no alternative but to send him to the local public high school.

That was where he came into his glory—not academically, he was never much one for cracking the books—but socially. He joined the football team, which gave him an outlet for some of his physical energies. He even became a star and was named to the all-county team two years in a row. But he decided to quit school two months before graduation and join the Navy. Of course, the girls continued to be all over him, especially now that he was almost six feet tall and better looking than ever. He had my mother's short curly hair, my father's green eyes but not his big hook nose. He knew how good-looking he was and used his looks to take advantage of every opportunity—except when it came to the serious matter of his future. In that matter he seemed downright self-destructive. Quitting school the way he did just a couple months before graduation was just one indication of it. Later, when he had the opportunity to marry into a good family with money, he turned his back on that as well, practically when he was halfway to the altar. To tell the truth, I don't think he would have been happy with her, and I say that despite the fact that she was my best friend. He seemed to have a talent for making the worst of his opportunities.

So, there we were, all six of us under the same roof again. Jack had been out of the service more than a year and had already broken his engagement to my friend when Donald returned from Korea. At that point, as far as I knew, Jack had no regular girlfriend. He was working for a local laundry, on the delivery truck, and of course made out like a bandit when it came to tips, especially at Christmas time. The women on his route used to wrap up their dirty laundry with pink ribbons and invite him in for a cup of tea when he brought it back the next day.

He loved telling stories about those lonely housewives. I can imagine what a thrill it must have been to see someone like Jack coming through their door in the middle of an otherwise dreary day. We were as amused by these stories as he was—Jack was, and is, a great storyteller—but looking back it seems a bit cruel to betray those women's confidences the way he did. After hours he hung out with his friends in one of the local bars, a saloon-cum-pizza on Lemoyne Avenue just across from the Fort Lee Diner. Weekends he went into Manhattan to the dances in Yorkville. He came home very late from those affairs.

Then one day the telephone started ringing and there was no one on the other end of the line. It didn't occur to me or anyone else the caller didn't want to talk to anyone but Jack. It would ring as much as half a dozen times during the course of an evening, and what with the claustrophobia we all were suffering as a result of living in such close quarters, those calls started to get on our nerves. There's something about a caller that doesn't answer when you pick up the phone that can drive you batty. It seemed to be getting on Jack's nerves especially, though at the time I never suspected anything was amiss. He flew off the handle more than once, even blaming the calls on Tommy, saying Tommy was too much of a coward to admit it.

It wasn't until several months later we found out, or at least were able to make a good guess, who was making those calls. The first I got wind of it was from my mother, and only then because I happened to walk in on a heated argument between herself and Jack when I came home from my job at the aluminum factory in Edgewater. By now Bobby and I could see the light at the end of the tunnel. I had already started to think about my wedding dress and to start discussions with my father about how much he could afford to spend on the wedding (it took him three years working overtime to pay it off, I will always be grateful to him for that).

Neither Jack nor my mother said anything to me afterward about the person who was making those calls. But the two of them sometimes went silent when I walked into the room, and it was obvious from the looks on their faces they had been involved in a very intense discussion. I assumed it had something to do with Jack's academic performance—he was attending night school at St. Peter's college in Jersey City thanks to the GI Bill, which was the same way my husband got his own education, and my brother was not always applying himself fully.

But I found out later that evening their talks had nothing to do with his education when my mother began snapping at me. I asked her what was wrong. She suddenly started crying and said Jack had gotten somebody pregnant but would not admit it and the girl's family were fit to be tied. Jack was out of the house at the time and my father had not yet come home from work. I didn't know what to say. I knew, of course, that Jack had played fast and lose all his life with the opposite sex, but for some reason it never occurred to me he could get himself into this kind of trouble. To tell you the truth, I was also a little hazy about how such things happened. I may have been twenty-three years old, but my sexual education was a bit behind today's average twelve-year-old. I tried to comfort my mother as best I could and assure her Jack would do the right thing. But having a stranger tell her that her son had impregnated her daughter and was denying responsibility for it was something that hit my mother hard. She's always been a woman who cared a great deal for her reputation (in the same breath claiming she doesn't give a tinker's dam what other people think of her). What was causing her so much grief was the shame that had been brought down on her for being the mother of a son who could behave in such an irresponsible manner. She was never ashamed of her husband that way despite the contempt she might hold him in for behaving as he did. But

Jack was the fruit of her womb. She felt responsible for what he did. It wasn't the worst thing in the world to get a woman pregnant—later on I learned there had been a number of illegitimate children in our family tree—but when something like that happened, the honorable thing, the only right thing, was to marry the girl or at least accept responsibility for the child. So far Jack had done nothing but deny everything, claiming the young woman had a reputation for consorting with men indiscriminately. How could she know if it was his child or someone else's?

Somehow during all of this I was supposed to make arrangements for my wedding. I always knew that one day I would be married in the old Madonna Church in West Fort Lee. Even when I had ideas about becoming a nun, they never displaced the dream I had of myself in a wedding gown standing next to my husband-to-be. In my earliest imaginings I couldn't see his face well enough to know who he was, but later on it was clearly Tim McCollough kneeling beside me at the altar. Now that the prospect of marriage was about to become a reality and I was confronted with all the details of planning a reception which I knew my father would have to go into hock for, that little girl's dream had turned into something more daunting. I've always been a bit high-strung, susceptible to uncontrollable bouts of crying, not just when things go wrong but for no reason at all. Once, I passed out at work sitting at my typewriter. The doctor diagnosed high blood pressure. The stresses and strains of preparing for my wedding, especially when the bridegroom was two thousand miles away, was enough for me to deal with without having to do so in the pressure cooker my home had become thanks to the carryings-on of my two brothers.

More than once the situation seemed more than I could deal with. What I wanted was to have my mother all to myself for those months leading up to the wedding. What girl wouldn't? There weren't just the practical matters to be attended to—and they were endless and legion—I also needed her support as a woman. I was very much in love with Bobby, but I knew next to nothing about making love the way a man and a wife make love. And, though I never expected my mother to go into graphic detail, I would have appreciated some general advice on the matter. As things turned out everything went fine. But I could have used some reinforcement, a bit of encouragement.

There were plenty of girls around whose experience was much wider than my own. I knew one of the things Bobby found attractive about me was that I had saved myself, not just in the technical sense of my virginity, but in not letting any boy go further than it was right for him to do. God knows I had my appetites even as a teenager but, thanks to the nuns, I knew right from wrong at an early age. I won't say I didn't go slightly over the line once or twice. When you're in love with a man it's very difficult not to give in to his urges, never mind your own. But I was content that I was able to present my husband with the sort of woman I knew he expected me to be on our wedding night.

It didn't occur to me in those days that I had a right to ask the same of him. I may have been innocent, but I was not so naive as not to have an inkling of what went on when soldiers went on leave in a place like El Paso. All of his letters were full of devotion, and in every one he renewed his vow of lifelong love. But I had been raised to look upon young men as inherently weaker than young women when it came to sex, and for that reason was prepared to make allowances for my fiancé that I could not make for myself. Some forty years later I have a different point of view. It seems to me now not so much that a young woman has a sexual drive that is less strong than a man's, or even that she is better able to control it. It's purely a question of practicality. A woman can get pregnant, a man cannot. That was, essentially, why the burden of chastity was laid on the shoulders of young women but not on young men like Bobby or my brother Jack.

So, when I heard Jack had gotten that woman pregnant my immediate reaction was that it must be the girl's fault. I had been taught it was always the girl's fault. Boys would be boys, men would be men. You couldn't expect them to control themselves, and given the opportunity—and God knew young women were willing to give him the opportunity—they would take it. I was even willing to accept his argument (though I never heard it from his own lips, we never discussed this episode in his life until many years later) that the young woman was promiscuous and could not really know who the father of the child was. In my imagined version of what happened, she had thrown herself at him as I had seen so many others do. I thought to myself, if I was a man and as attractive to the opposite sex as he was, would I be able to resist the temptation? I never thought for a moment he had not sinned in accepting her favors, but sin was something we were all subject to, and sexual sin was virtually unavoidable for young men.

Eventually my mother and I discussed his situation candidly. In a way, it was a relief for me because it took my mind off the anxieties of my impending matrimony. I still took my moral cues very much from her in those days, and I sensed she was of two minds about where Jack's responsibility lay. On the one hand, she realized the young woman's supposed promiscuity left the paternity of the child in question. But the very fact that Jack admitted to having sexual relations with her made him the father as likely as anyone else, and the idea that my mother might have a grandchild who would be unacknowledged and perhaps ill-cared-for tormented her.

I don't think that as a young woman my mother ever wanted a family the way I did. Child-rearing was an obligation for her, one she accepted willingly but not one she had looked forward to with the kind of enthusiasm I felt. I suppose this was the result of her having been saddled with the partial raising of her brothers, not to mention my father's gallivanting ways when the three of us were still young. Nevertheless, once a baby came into the picture it didn't matter to her whether the child was legitimate or illegitimate, planned or unplanned, or even black or white. She could not bear the thought of it not being properly cared for. The many Catholic missionary orders she supported over the years are testimony to this. She still gets solicitations from the Salesians and others, not to mention Protestant and even Jewish organizations. If a picture of a starving child is enclosed, it's dollars to doughnuts she'll send a check.

So you can imagine how she felt when it seemed possible her own flesh and blood, once removed, was about to come into the world without a father and left to a fate that would be beyond her power to do anything about. One afternoon I walked into her bedroom and found her sitting by the window staring out at the leaves falling from the trees that separated our apartment from the private homes on Hunter Avenue. She was crying. She must have been sitting there for a while because her eyes were red and the tears even seemed to have inflamed her cheeks. She was constantly dabbing at them with a tissue that she kept scrunched up in her hand. She always had one of those tissues on her person somewhere, usually in the pocket of her housecoat or up the sleeve of her dress.

I asked what was the matter, though I already had a pretty good idea. Even so, her husband still gave her a lot of grief. She might just as well have been crying for that reason as any other. As I've said, I was desperate for maternal attention to alleviate the anxiety that was growing stronger each day as my wedding grew closer. Even so, I could never bear to see my mother cry. I would rather have taken upon myself the cause of her grief than see her face disfigured that way. I put my arm around her as if it were I who were the mother and asked, "What is it?"

For a moment she said nothing, staring out at the brown leaves as if my words had not registered. But when she started to speak I realized her reluctance to answer was because she didn't want to lose whatever self-control she was managing to maintain. But the strain of holding it in finally became too much. She broke down and wept with a lack of restraint I've rarely seen her subject to, a couple notable exceptions being the day she received news that Donald had been wounded in Korea and the day we buried her last child, a badly malformed infant that was the result of a tranquilizer her doctor had prescribed during that pregnancy. "I can't seem to do a damned thing right," she managed to get out between sobs.

I started crying myself. I've never been able to hold back tears when I see someone else crying, especially if I see their grief is genuine. My mother never cried for any other reason. She was entirely without the kind of guile some women use to get their way. I was also crying for pity. She felt responsible not just for what Jack had done but also for Donald's behavior, not to mention the rotten state of her own marriage—or what I believed to be its rotten state in those days, I have since come to believe that however desperate and dysfunctional my parents' union once seemed to me, they had some kind of arrangement that worked well enough for them.

She pulled herself together. It was as if my embrace, at least during the first few seconds when she had seemed to welcome it, suddenly roused her. She scraped at her eyes with that sodden tissue, looked around as if wondering how she had ended up by that window in the first place and said, "What time is it? Jesus, Mary and Joseph, and here I don't have dinner on yet."

XVI

By the time we arrive home the sun has begun to set. Not that we have ever seen the sun drop below the horizon in that part of town. But the summer twilight is long and gentle, easily the best part of the day. I love to ramble through it, gathering grasshoppers from the tall grass behind the lilac bushes at the back of our yard or playing hide-and-seek with the few other children in the neighborhood. For me it is twilight, not dawn, when the world seems fresh and new and full of possibility. Even the sparrows' irritable chatter as they bed down for the night in the ivy of the brick house next to our own seems like the good-natured quarreling of children in a morning schoolyard.

The cab driver has had to help my mother extricate my father from the back seat where he fell into a deep stupor as soon as we reached the Manhattan approach to the George Washington Bridge. He manages to make it to the front stoop before collapsing and going back to sleep, his head resting on the pink brick at an angle that makes it look as if he has broken his neck.

"Get up, John," my mother says, quietly at first, her face red from the heat and the exertion of getting him across the sidewalk.

He doesn't move, his mouth half-open, a bead of drool hanging from the corner of his thick bottom lip. I see her anger rising as she moves closer to him, but despite what he has put her through it does not seem reasonable to me to expect a man to a obey a request he is incapable of hearing.

She prods the shoulder of his white, short-sleeve shirt cautiously as if he were a dangerous animal that might suddenly spring at her. When his flesh fails to respond she pushes again more forcefully, then again, until his head is rocking back and forth. It is like watching someone abuse a dead man.

"Wake up, John!" she says, her voice no longer a whisper, though still subdued for the neighbors' sake. "Wake up!"

Eventually he stirs, not like someone roused from a drunken stupor but with the determination of a soul called to resurrection by a heavenly host. His drooling mouth snaps shut. One eye twitches but does not open all the way until my mother administers another shove.

"For the love of God, John! Get up!"

His hands reach for purchase on the brick steps even before he seems to know where he is. After great effort he achieves an upright state.

"Don't just sit there for all the neighbors to see. Get in the house."

But he is conscious enough to distinguish now between the call to judgment and his wife's nagging. His high brow creases in irritation. "I'm going, Mary. Just give me a minute."

A "minute" being the one thing he can never get from this woman or her pesky emissaries. A "minute" to finish his beer in peace. A "minute" to rouse his flesh to action after a long, hard day of drinking. The world seemed to be ever conspiring to rob him of his "minutes," not just his wife but me too when I have to use the toilet and he is already in there enjoying a smoke and the sports pages of the *Journal American;* the "minute" when he wants to linger over his dessert and my sister — another of his wife's minions — intent on clearing the table removes the food from under his nose. "A minute" seems to sum up all he has so modestly asked of life. A moment to himself. Is that so much? I can't see why my mother or sister — or myself, for that matter, no matter how full my bladder — can't allow him this modest indulgence, forgetting, in the way I have of taking everyone literally, that his "minutes" never do come singly but seriatim and without limit like the revolutions of the big clock on the kitchen wall.

But up he gets finally, as though raising not just mortal flesh but a pack of invisible powers that are attached to it. At the top of the stoop he stumbles, then sways to and fro as if about to topple backward and dash his brains out on the pink bricks, all his minutes gone forever. I can't tell for sure if his unsteadiness is genuine or another of his tricks, a clown's antics on the high wire as thousands laugh and gasp far below—clowns in fact being my father's favorite form of entertainment.

Somehow he makes it into the front porch where he collapses alongside the green table on whose surface I have played so many games of Cargoes and Monopoly. My mother and I step around him, first making sure the screen door is closed so his comatose body is not visible to passersby.

Supper will be a bowl of Cheerios, but that will come later, after I have walked off the hamburgers and sodas I consumed that afternoon. In the meantime I am free to ramble about the neighborhood, enjoying the remains of the day. There is a giant pear tree, big as a mature oak, in the middle of a circular drive just behind those lilac bushes at the back of our yard. It belongs to a Masonic lodge that fronts on Main Street. Lodge members sometimes let us watch a baseball game on their seven-inch black-and-white. My mother has told me the Masons are an anti-Catholic organization and that all American presidents are automatically elevated to the thirty-second degree when they take the oath of office. But I either have trouble making the connection between this insidious plot against the true church and the sweet hard fruit that grows in such abundance in their backyard, or I see my taking of the fruit as retribution for their perfidy. The lower branches are low enough for me to grab hold of if I stand on tiptoe. When I shake them a shower of brown pears falls to the ground, an abundance that allows me to select only the best unblemished ones, a profligacy from which I sample, discard, take a bite from another, then throw away like a mighty pasha who has all the riches of his realm at his command. Despite what my mother has told me about the Masons', she has never designated this particular tree as one from which I must not eat. So I gather its bounty shamelessly, wantonly, checked only by a lodge member if he happens to spot what I am doing.

Despite the orgy of drunkenness I have witnessed that afternoon and the wages of suffering my mother has been forced to pay for it, the world I wander through this last delightful hour of the day, blithely crossing from yard to yard as if there are no — and never have been – individual, never mind national borders, this world of green lawn and golden light seems untouched by Adam's sin and its consequences. I traverse it as a child of nature, one of those South Sea islanders I see in movies, untainted by any sense of wrong-doing, free to do as I please.

As the waning light turns to deep amber I come upon Carol Grimes, a girl two years older than me who lives with her mother and younger brother above a tavern on Main Street next to the remains of an abandoned movie theater (Fort Lee won't have its own working movie house until I am ten years old). I invite her to join me in the low shed beneath the front porch where my father stores bags of cement, sand and the occasional two-by-four. With its small door closed, the shed is the darkest place on earth. To see at all we have to leave it open a fraction of an inch. But seeing is what I very much want, the reason why I have brought Carol there. I drop the rubber suspenders from my shoulders and pull down my pants and underpants. For a moment Carol stares at my erect organ as if I were showing her an interesting birthmark. But then she smiles and hikes her skirt high above her waist, exposing white cotton panties.

Her plump bottom looks as inviting as a bowl of my mother's cake batter. I ask her to sit on my face and she obliges happily, taking care not to put her full weight on me. It does not occur to me that my father is still lying in an alcoholic coma on the floor of the front porch just above our heads. He is as far from my thoughts now as are the sweet pears on the tree behind the Masonic lodge or the events of that long afternoon in Manhattan and Queens. The cheeks of Carol Grimes' soft white bottom are all I care about, and the indifference with which she gently lowers and raises and then lowers them again fills me with a holy delight.

Thomas J. Hubschman is the author of Look at Me Now, My Bess, Billy Boy, The Jew's Wife & Other Stories, Song of the Mockingbird and three science fiction novels. His stories and essays have appeared in numerous print and online publications. Two of his short stories were broadcast on the BBC World Service. He has edited two anthologies of new writing from Africa, Asia and the Caribbean.

If you enjoyed Beer, please leave a brief review at the site where you purchased it. Thank you.

www.ingramcontent.com/pod-product-compliance
Lightning Source LLC
Chambersburg PA
CBHW031128210626
46816CB00015B/1236